"I Hate Being Attracted To You."

Kyle's gaze stormed hers, as fierce as a silent war cry.

Joyce struggled to contain her emotions, to stop herself from tasting every inch of him. "Then get off me."

"I don't want to." He traced her top, running his fingers along the neckline. He moved lower, righting her clothes, respecting her in a way she'd never imagined. "And you don't want me to, either."

Like a heart-pounding fool, she let him stay there, body to body, breath to breath. Even so, she fought the urge to put her arms around him, to hold him. She'd known him for eight months, almost long enough to have a baby.

That alone scared the death out of her. Her biological clock wouldn't stop ticking.

"We're in trouble."

Dear Reader

Silhouette Desire has a fantastic selection of novels for you this month, starting with our latest DYNASTIES: THE ASHTONS title, *Condition of Marriage* by Emilie Rose. Pregnant by one man...married to another, sounds like another Ashton scandal to me! *USA TODAY* bestselling author Peggy Moreland is back with a brand-new TANNERS OF TEXAS story. In *Tanner Ties*, it's a female Tanner who is looking for answers...and finds romance instead.

Our TEXAS CATTLEMAN'S CLUB: THE SECRET DIARY also continues this month with Brenda Jackson's fabulous *Strictly Confidential Attraction*, the story of a shy secretary who gets the chance to play house with her supersexy boss. Sheri WhiteFeather returns with another sexy Native American hero. You fell for Kyle in Sheri's previous Silhouette Bombshell novel, but just wait until you get to really know him in *Apache Nights*.

Two compelling miniseries also continue this month: Linda Conrad's *Reflected Pleasures*, the second book in THE GYPSY INHERITANCE—a family with a legacy full of surprises. And Bronwyn Jameson's PRINCES OF THE OUTBACK series has its second installment with *The Rich Stranger*—a man who must produce an heir in order to maintain his fortune.

Here's hoping this September's selections give you all the romance, all the drama and all the sensationalism you've come to expect from Silhouette Desire.

Melissa Jeglinski

Melissa Jeglinski
Senior Editor
Silhouette Desire

Please address questions and book requests to:
Silhouette Reader Service
U.S.: 3010 Walden Ave., P.O. Box 1325, Buffalo, NY 14269
Canadian: P.O. Box 609, Fort Erie, Ont. L2A 5X3

APACHE NIGHTS

SHERI WHITEFEATHER

Silhouette®

Desire

Published by Silhouette Books

America's Publisher of Contemporary Romance

SILHOUETTE BOOKS

ISBN 0-373-76678-5

APACHE NIGHTS

Books by Sheri WhiteFeather

Silhouette Desire

Warrior's Baby #1248
Skyler Hawk: Lone Brave #1272
Jesse Hawk: Brave Father #1278
Cheyenne Dad #1300
Night Wind's Woman #1332
Tycoon Warrior #1364
Cherokee #1376
Comanche Vow #1388
Cherokee Marriage Dare #1478
Sleeping with Her Rival #1496
Cherokee Baby #1509
Cherokee Dad #1523
The Heart of a Stranger #1527
Cherokee Stranger #1563
A Kept Woman #1575
Steamy Savannah Nights #1597
Betrayed Birthright #1663
Apache Nights #1678

Silhouette Bombshell

Always Look Twice #27

Silhouette Books

Dynasties: Summer in Savannah
"The Dare Affair"

SHERI WHITEFEATHER

lives in Southern California and enjoys ethnic dining, attending powwows and visiting art galleries and vintage clothing stores near the beach. Since her one true passion is writing, she is thrilled to be part of the Silhouette Desire line. When she isn't writing, she often reads until the wee hours of the morning.

Sheri's husband, a member of the Muscogee Creek Nation, inspires many of her stories. They have a son, a daughter and a trio of cats—domestic and wild. She loves to hear from her readers. You may write to her at: P.O. Box 17146, Anaheim, California 92817. Visit her Web site at www.SheriWhiteFeather.com.

To the readers who noticed Kyle in *Always Look Twice*
and asked if I was going to write his story,
this book is for you.

One

Where in the hell was he?

Joyce Riggs waited at the locked gate in front of Kyle Prescott's obscure seven-acre dwelling, with an irate rottweiler snarling at her through the chain-link fence.

The guard dog fit Kyle to a T, but so did the other pooch, a miniature dachshund, keeping the rotten rotty company.

How many people would pair a rottweiler and an itty-bitty wiener dog together in the same yard?

And speaking of the yard…

Scattered car parts. Old lawn furniture. Play-ground equipment. Wagon wheels. A cast-iron stove.

She blinked, deciding it was impossible to item-ize everything. Kyle was, after all, a junk dealer. Or at least that was his legitimate profession, his cover, the work he claimed on his income tax returns.

She knew he was a militant who trained other mil-itants, a Native American activist who kept the au-thorities guessing. And to make matters worse, she had a crush on him, an irritating attraction that had been nipping at her heels since they'd both decided nearly eight months ago that they despised each other.

She blew out a rough breath and did her damned-est to ignore the salivating rotty. But it wasn't easy. The domineering beast was getting angrier by the second. The wiener dog, on the other hand, was grin-ning at her like a sweet little goon.

Finally a banging sound caught her attention. The snap of a heavy wooden door, no doubt. Both dogs reacted, and like a muscle-bound mirage, Kyle ap-peared in the distance, descending the porch steps of his ancient home.

He lived in an isolated section of the high desert where Charles Manson and his merry band of mur-derers had been rumored to spend time, a place that still seemed like *Helter Skelter* to the average fear-abiding citizen.

Kyle moved closer, and Joyce squinted at him, wishing he didn't make her pulse flip and flutter.

It took a while, but he reached the gate, emphasizing his long, lazy strides. And then he smirked, giving her a roguish, Rhett Butler-type look. The rottweiler was still baring his fangs, growling in the name of his gorgeous master. She could tell the dog was male. She could see his I'm-a-boy testes.

Fiddle-dee-dee, she thought. Supposedly Kyle had quite a pair, too. Not to mention the body part that went with them. She'd heard he was hung like a Trojan horse.

Not that she cared.

"Detective Riggs," he said. "What a surprise."

"I called and told you to expect me."

"And I told you not to bother."

"Aren't you the least bit curious why I'm here?" she baited.

He angled his head. As usual, his razor-sharp shoulder length hair was held in place with a cloth headband, reminiscent of the Geronimo era in Apache history. At six-four, he was a tall, dark half-blood, a man who carried his heritage like a nine-teenth-century rifle.

He wore a blue T-shirt, button-fly jeans and knee-high moccasins. He was thirty-six, the same age as Joyce, but they didn't have anything in common, nothing but an unyielding attraction.

He shifted his stance, and the sandy soil settled around his feet. "If this is official police business then you'll have to get a warrant."

"Why?" The October wind snapped like a whip, stinging her face. "Did you kill someone?"

His smirk faded. Kyle was a highly decorated Desert Storm soldier, a full-blown war hero. He didn't take death lightly. But neither did she. Joyce was a homicide detective.

For an instant, they simply stared at each other, trapped in a challenging moment. Then she glanced at the rottweiler. He remained on teeth-gnashing alert. "Will you call off that damn dog?"

The smile returned, the crisscross pattern on the fence distorting Kyle's handsome features. "He doesn't like cops."

"I doubt he likes anyone."

"He likes Olivia."

Trust Kyle to bring up his former lover. Olivia was a mutual friend, a psychic who assisted the LAPD and the FBI and every other law enforcement agency Kyle claimed to hate.

But Olivia was also a beautiful, strong-willed woman who trained with Kyle in his private compound, something Joyce was hoping to do.

Especially now, while she was desperate to piece her shattered emotions back together.

"I'm willing to pay you," she said.

That caught his attention. He gave the dog a subtle command, and it stopped snarling. He'd spoken in what sounded like a foreign language. Not anything Joyce recognized. Most likely, he'd trained his rotty to respond to Apache.

"Pay me for what?" he asked.

"For your sessions. Hand to hand combat. War games. Everything you offer here."

"I don't train cops."

"Then I'll be your first."

He gave her a suspicious glare. "Why?"

"Because I'm going through a tough time, some personal issues I can't seem to resolve." She didn't like revealing herself to him, but she wasn't going to unearth every little detail. Joyce's biological clock was ready to explode, something she couldn't begin to understand, something that was spinning out of control. "I need to blow off some steam. Get physical. Take my mind off my problems."

"Then go to the police range and fire your gun. Do whatever your kind do."

"My kind?" She wanted to kick him through the fence, but she knew the rottweiler would go nuts if she staged an attack. "Quit hiding behind your dog and let me in."

"Nice try, Detective. But I'm not macho enough to fall for that."

Yeah, right. He was as macho as a modern-day warrior could get. "Olivia told me all about you, Kyle. Everything."

He had the gall to grin. "So you know I'm good

in bed. So what?" He paused, looked her up and down. "Is that why you're really here, Detective? To bang my brains out?"

She roamed her gaze over him, giving him a taste of his own chauvinistic medicine. "What brains?"

He almost laughed. Almost. But not quite.

As for her, she was used to sparring with hard-edged men, with criminals, with other detectives. Being a woman in a male-dominated environment made her stronger.

But sometimes it made her lonely, too.

A second later, Kyle surprised her by unlocking the gate. "You can come in if you want to."

She motioned to the rottweiler. "What about him?"

"Clyde won't hurt you. Not unless I tell him to."

Clyde. She glanced at the sturdy black and tan canine. He didn't move a well-toned muscle. He sat like a statue at his master's feet. She scanned the grounds for the dachshund and couldn't help but smile. The little wiener dog was wiggling like a ballpark frank trying to escape from a bun.

"What's that one's name?" she asked.

Kyle's lips quirked. "Bonnie."

She raised her eyebrows. Bonnie and Clyde. He'd named his dogs after bank robbers.

He rattled the gate. "Are you coming in or not?"

Suddenly a voice in her head told her to go home, to stay away from Kyle Prescott. But the need to fight her way out of her problems, to train with him, kept her grounded.

Besides, he didn't have a record. And although his activities often bordered on the suspicious, Joyce wanted to believe that when the chips were down, he could be trusted. On the day they'd met, he'd helped the LAPD apprehend a killer, a case that involved Native witchcraft. Of course, he'd only done that for Olivia, for a woman who'd fallen in love with someone else. Not that Olivia had ever been in love with Kyle. She'd claimed he was a bit too bizarre to make her feel secure.

Nonetheless, Joyce took a chance and stepped onto his property. Instantly he moved forward and snapped the padlock back into place, locking her into his domain, telling her, without words, that it was too late to turn tail and run.

As if he could scare her off. She wouldn't dream of chickening out, even if the rational voice in her head was calling her an idiot.

When he turned away from her, she noticed the small-of-the-back holster attached to his belt. She glanced at the semiautomatic SIG and wondered if he armed himself every morning. She knew darn well that Kyle didn't have a permit to carry a gun, open or concealed, but he was on his own property and that put him within the limits of the law.

"Expecting some bad guys to show up?" she asked.

"Just a bad girl." He caught sight of her holstered gun, too. "But she's already here."

"Touché."

"It was your idea to invade my world." He motioned to his house. "Want some coffee?"

"As long as you don't poison it."

"My coffee *is* poison."

And so were his pheromones, she thought. The sparks he sent flying, the sexual energy that made him seem like a predator.

She walked beside him, and Clyde fell into step. She could tell the rotty was aware of everything she did. But so was Kyle.

Refusing to give the males too much attention, she focused on Bonnie. The sweet little thing tagged along, her low-slung belly nearly dragging on the ground.

As they continued toward the house, as Bonnie skirted around salvage items that got in her way, Joyce studied the outbuildings on Kyle's property.

"Is that where you store the rest of your merchandise?" she asked.

He followed her line of sight, then nodded. "Furniture, collectables, memorabilia. Things you'd find in trading posts and antique stores. I've got some nice pieces for sale." He paused. "Do you like vintage stuff?"

"Yes." She loved browsing in charming old stores,

shopping for rare finds. "But atmosphere is important to me, too."

He made a grand gesture. "You don't think my place has atmosphere?"

Was he joking? She couldn't quite tell. "Your airplane hangar has appeal." The enormous structure sat behind everything else, taking up ten thousand square feet of space. She knew the building had been modified to support a highly sophisticated laser tag course, a compound she was anxious to see. But he still hadn't agreed to train her.

To help her with her cause.

To battle the emotions that threatened to swallow her.

Kyle slanted the lady cop a sideways glance. He intended to grill her, to figure out if she was on the level. For all he knew, she'd heard about his upcoming mission and wanted to poke her investigator's nose into his business.

He studied her profile, the chin-length sweep of blond hair, the simple curve of feminine eyelashes. This wasn't a case for a homicide detective. He didn't plan on hurting anyone—no guns, no knives, no weapons of choice. But what he intended to do was still illegal, and Joyce could easily turn him over to one of her peers.

But as far as he was concerned, his mission was

sacred, a spiritual issue, something that was worth going to jail for. Even dying for, if it came down to that.

Of course, neither of those risks appealed to him. And neither did Joyce involving herself in his affairs.

Within minutes, they reached his house. After taking the weather-beaten steps, he opened the front door, gesturing for her to enter. She went inside, the dogs trailing after her.

She glanced around his living room and made a face. "Olivia warned me that you weren't much of a housekeeper. But this looks like somebody ransacked the place."

Typical, he thought. Females always grumbled about the clutter in which he lived, including his former bedmate, a woman who'd accused him of being the biggest slob on the planet.

But he didn't care. He'd decorated with an eclectic style of furniture, with vintage pieces from different eras. And yeah, it was messy, with books, magazines and old clothes littering almost every surface. But he liked it that way. It kept his lovers from getting domestic ideas about him.

"Are you ready to get grossed out by my kitchen?" he asked.

"Is it that bad?"

"You'll probably think so."

Sure enough, she did. When they rounded the corner, the dogs in silent pursuit, she wrinkled her nose. "This is beyond gross."

Kyle merely shrugged. The food-encrusted plates in the sink were probably growing mold. But he had lots of extra dinnerware, boxes and boxes of second-hand stuff. When his dishes got too disgusting, he threw them away and started over. The same with pots, pans, glasses and flatware. The whole shebang.

"Is the coffeepot clean?" she asked.

"It's new." He plugged in the reconditioned unit and set about to make a dark, Colombian brew. He kept hundreds of preowned machines on hand. "Or sort of new. I've never used it before."

"Thank God."

He spared her a quick glance. He suspected that she lived in a tidy West L.A apartment, with silk flowers and a concrete balcony. Pretty but practical. Just like her.

While the coffee brewed, he leaned against the counter and took the time to check her out, to analyze her appearance. Neatly styled hair, blue eyes, noteworthy bone structure and minimal makeup. As for her clothes, she'd chosen an average white blouse, a lightweight blazer and black slacks.

Conservative, he thought. Coplike.

But damn if she didn't have a stimulating body, toned and athletic. Her mouth aroused him, too. The pillowy fullness, the insatiable, go-down-on-a-guy shape. He'd heard that she had a teasing nature. That she flirted for the fun of it. Of course, he'd never seen that side of her.

He wondered how she would look in a push-up bra, smoky eyeliner and stiletto heels. Incredible, he decided.

She glared at him. "Cut it out."

"Cut what out?"

"Looking at me like that."

"Like what?"

"A Cro-Magnon."

Amused, he bit back a smile. Clyde was watching her with guard dog awareness, and Bonnie was sniffing at her nondescript shoes. "Cro-Magnon men were capable hunters and food gatherers. Artistic cave painters, too."

"You know darn well I was referring to their sexual habits."

"Dragging womenfolk off by their hair? It's a fascinating theory, but I don't think it's true. Homo sapiens weren't dim-witted brutes. They were much more sophisticated than—"

She cut him off, and Bonnie scampered away. "Are you denying that you were getting hot and bothered over me?"

"No." He wasn't denying anything. "I was picturing you as a femme fatale." He gave her clothes an unappreciative wave. "You could use a makeover."

"Really?" She gave his duds the same distasteful treatment. "Well, so could you." She tilted her head, as if she were recreating him in her mind. "I guess that means I'll have to picture you in a suit and tie."

Kyle cringed, then turned to pour the coffee. He wouldn't be caught dead in a suit. If his family buried him in one, he would come back to haunt them. "You date corporate guys?"

"They're the type I prefer." She glanced at the cup he'd given her. "Do you have sugar?"

"No."

"Cream? Milk?"

"Milk. But I'm not willing to share. There's only a little bit left and I'm saving it for my cereal, for tomorrow's breakfast."

She returned the coffee. "You're a terrible host."

He pushed the cup back at her, maneuvering the pitch-black drink between them. "I never offered you anything but poison. Besides you deserve it for trying to dress me in a suit."

"And what do you deserve for trying to put me in a G-string and thigh-high hose?"

"Not bad, Detective." She'd almost got it right. "But it was a padded bra and spiked heels."

"I wasn't wearing a skimpy thong?"

"No." He leveled his gaze. "You weren't wearing anything down there."

The coffee sloshed over the side of her cup, nearly

burning both of their hands. She flinched, but he didn't move. He'd just taken control. He'd rattled her senses.

She regained her composure. "I should drag you off by your hair. Pull it out of that perverted skull of yours."

"Now that I'd like to see." He stood right where he was, challenging her to make the first move. She glanced at the rottweiler, and Kyle gave her a half-cocked smile. She would pay hell to get past his dog. Or him for that matter. She might be a highly effective cop, a Special Section detective who tracked serial killers and worked on high profile cases, but she'd come to him for training, for force-on-force drills, for the fight that was supposedly raging in her blood. No matter what, they both knew his tactical skills outmatched hers. His specialty was close-quarter combat, battlefield techniques perfected by the U.S. Special Forces, U.S. Army Rangers and U.S. Marine Corps.

"Is that spiel you gave me true?" he asked.

"What spiel?"

He set her coffee on the counter. "That bit about you going through a tough time. About having personal problems you can't resolve."

"I wasn't lying."

Although she glanced away, something flashed in her eyes. Confusion, he thought. She appeared to be at war with herself.

Were her problems real? Or was she a skilled actress?

He pushed her further, looking for answers. "Did someone hurt you? Is that what's wrong?"

"No."

"You didn't get in too deep with some guy? With some jerk who screwed you over?" He knew there were men who took advantage, who made promises they didn't keep. But Kyle wasn't one of them. His relationships never went beyond sex, beyond raw, honest urges.

"There's no one," she told him. "It isn't like that."

"Then what's going on?"

"Nothing I care to talk about." Her chest rose and fell, her breathing accelerated, just a little, just enough for him to notice.

She wasn't acting, he decided. She was putting herself on the line, something he doubted she did very often. He couldn't imagine what kinds of problems a tough-willed detective like her couldn't resolve. It made him hungry to kiss her, to taste her confusion, to let her seduce him. But he wasn't about to break his self-imposed code.

He didn't sleep with white women.

Of course that didn't mean he wasn't going to help her. Joyce had come to him for a legitimate reason.

He turned away. "I'll get the milk for your coffee."

She blinked. "Are you calling a truce?"

"I'm just trying to be a halfway decent host." He went to the refrigerator, removed the carton and gave Clyde a silent signal, letting the dog know the upcoming threat wouldn't be real. "I'm going to train you."

"You are?" She accepted the milk and poured it into her cup. "What's your schedule like?"

"I'll have to check my calendar."

She glanced up. "I've got time off this week. Or is that too soon for you?"

"I'll try to work something out," he told her, even though he'd already worked it out.

She stirred her coffee, and he curbed a carnivorous smile.

Joyce's first session and the surprise attack that went with it was about to begin.

Two

Joyce sipped her coffee. It was strong, but it was far from poisonous. "This is actually pretty good."

"Glad you think so." He came forward, taking the hot drink from her hand. "Too bad you won't get to finish it."

"What you are doing?"

"This." He set her cup on the counter and moved even closer.

Too close, she thought. She could smell the soap on his skin. An outdoorsy scent, a blend of lavender and sage, of man and nature.

She met his gaze and noticed the brown and gold pattern. Tiger's-eye, she thought. Like the quartz stone Roman soldiers used to wear to protect them in battle.

He moistened his lips, and her pulse went haywire. Was he going to kiss her?

She knew she shouldn't let him. But she was curious to taste him. One long, lingering jolt. One forbidden flavor.

When he pinned her against the counter, she lifted her chin, daring him to do it, to take her mouth with his.

But he didn't. He grabbed her gun instead.

Son of a bitch.

She tried to stop him, but within seconds he'd confiscated her 9mm and ditched it, right along with the SIG he carried. Both guns went sliding across the vinyl floor, out of sight and out of reach. This wasn't an armed battle. This was street fighting, a down-and-dirty brawl.

Only he wasn't hurting her. If anything, she was simply being restrained.

She knew how to punch, how to kick, how land well-aimed blows. But her moves didn't work on him.

Joyce gritted her teeth and attempted a stomp that was supposed to bring down a giant, someone as big as Kyle.

For all the good it did.

He took her down instead. "You're blowing it, Detective."

He landed on top of her, nailing her to the floor.

He kept her there, under him, his tiger's-eye eyes boring into hers. She couldn't move her arms; she couldn't even lift her pelvis a fraction.

But the weight of his body felt good.

Much too good.

"Get off me, Kyle."

He didn't listen. He continued looking at her. Was this another trick? At this point, she still wanted him to kiss her. Softly. Gently. Yet she wanted to shred his clothes, too. To snap and bite and leave marks on his soap-scented skin.

Nothing in her brain made any sense.

"Tell me what's wrong." He climbed off her, ending the exercise, freeing her from his bond. "Tell me what's going on in your life."

Caught off guard, she sat up and noticed he was sitting on the floor, too. "We already discussed that."

"And you didn't tell me a thing."

"It's personal." She wasn't about to admit that her biological clock was ticking like a bomb. For Joyce, it wasn't a natural feeling. She hated the nesting urges inside her, the marriage/baby lust interfering with her job, with everything that used to make her happy. Being a wife and mother had never been part of her agenda. Yet it had begun to take over, like a horror-movie body snatcher.

"Are you sure it's something you can fight your way out of?" he asked.

"Yes." It had to be, she thought. Because she didn't intend to let those urges destroy her. Nor did she intend to cater to them, to marry the first romantic bonehead that came along and have his babies.

Speaking of boneheads...

Kyle stretched his legs and tapped the soles of her shoes with his. "Are you impressed?"

"With what?" She pushed back, pressing on his knee-high moccasins. They held no adornment. No fringe, no tiny beading, no colorful paint. "You?"

"I stole your gun, cop-girl."

"And you can return it now, cheater-boy."

"I didn't cheat."

Joyce couldn't believe they were playing footsies, flirting like a couple of middle school kids. She tried to quit, but he continued, so she did too, kicking him a little harder. "You pretended you were going to kiss me."

"It's not my fault you fell for that."

No, it was hers. And she wouldn't let it happen again.

Suddenly he stopped moving and said something in what she assumed was Apache. She frowned at him, then realized he was talking to Clyde. The dog came forward and dropped her gun in her lap.

She glanced at the handle of the 9mm. The rotty had slobbered all over it. "Gee, thanks."

Kyle grinned. "Wanna know where mine is?"

"Up your butt?" she asked and made him chuckle.

"It's in my holster. Right where it should be." He attacked her soles again. "Tricky, aren't I?"

Joyce couldn't decide if he was a militant or a magician. She moved her feet away from his, then wiped the handle of her gun with her blouse. "That was a lousy training session. All you did was show off."

"I was assessing your skills."

"Fine. Whatever." She wasn't about to throw in the towel. "I better get more out of the next session."

"You will." He stood and offered her hand. "Come by tomorrow around noon."

"You better be worth the money." She refused his hand, hating that he'd bested her. Not in a fight. But in that nonexistent kiss.

The strategy he'd used against her.

After Joyce left, Kyle drove his Jeep to Olivia's downtown loft. He didn't like going to other people for help, but he didn't have a choice. Besides, Olivia was a friend, or as close to a friend as a female could get.

Women were a strange breed. He appreciated their bodies. He considered them the Creator's most compelling work of art, but he didn't understand their minds. And Joyce was no exception. She baffled the hell out of him.

Edgy, he sat on Olivia's sofa. She was perched on

the chair across from him, waiting for him to speak. He used to call her Liv, but he'd decided to stop using the nickname, to stop being overly familiar with her, especially now that she was sleeping with someone else.

She crossed her legs, and he noticed her short black skirt and fishnet stockings. Olivia had always dressed like a dominatrix. Her naughty style is what had attracted him to her. That, and her Lakota/Apache blood.

"Do you know what's going on with Joyce?" he asked.

She ran her hand through her hair. She wore it short and choppy. Her lips were a bold shade of red and her eyes were rimmed in a smudgy kohl liner. "Going on how?"

"With her personal life."

"She doesn't confide in me."

"No girl talk?"

"No."

He blew out an irritated-sounding breath, letting his former lover know that he didn't believe her. He'd always heard that women stuck together. That they chattered like gossip-addicted magpies. "You told her stuff about me."

"So?"

"So did you tell her I was hot in bed?" He sure as hell hoped so, or else he would look like a fool, considering he'd already bragged to Joyce and accused her of wanting him.

"Of course I did. It's the only thing you're good at."

He wasn't flattered, not completely. He took pride in other aspects of his life, in the Warrior Society that dictated his missions. "I'm good at other things."

"You were a lousy boyfriend."

Okay, so she had him there. He hadn't mastered the art of romance, of wining and dining. And he totally sucked at the emotional stuff. But he'd never claimed to be polished or poetic.

"Who cares?" he said.

"Apparently you do or you wouldn't be asking me about Joyce."

"I was asking about her personal problems." The mystery of why she was troubled was driving him crazy. "She came to me for training. She wants to fight her way out of her dilemma."

"I know. She told me."

"Right." He gave Olivia a hard stare. "During the conversation that wasn't girl talk." To him, evaluating a man's performance in bed was as girly as a discussion could get, even if the man in question was grateful for it. "I can't believe she didn't go into more detail. That she didn't admit what's bothering her."

"Well, she didn't."

They both fell silent. Frustrated, Kyle looked around the loft. The walls were decorated with a mural Olivia's sister had painted, with fantasy creatures that included an armor-clad knight and a fire-breathing dragon.

He squinted at the knight and wondered if there was a damsel in distress waiting in the wings somewhere.

If women like Olivia and Joyce ruled the world, they would be slaying the dragon. Not that Kyle didn't respect ass-kicking females. They totally turned him on. But he appreciated their softer sides, too. The vulnerability that made them women. Which, he supposed, was why Joyce's secret was chipping away at him.

He picked up a decorative pillow and fussed with the froufrou tassel, flicking the gold fringe. "Why didn't you try to zap into Joyce's mind and pick her brain? Why didn't you try to find out what's going on?"

Olivia glanced at the front door. "I wasn't going to invade her privacy. That wouldn't have been right."

Right, smight. Kyle wished he were psychic.

Just then, the door opened and a dark-haired man in a black suit entered the trendy building and set his briefcase down. Olivia must have sensed his presence.

Special Agent Ian West. Her FBI lover. She stood and West came toward her. They didn't say anything. They locked lips instead, sweet and slow, as if they hadn't seen each other for a thousand years. But that wasn't the case. They worked together as often as they could, and whenever the hotshot profiler was in town, he crashed at her place.

When the other man deepened the kiss, Kyle made a disgusted face. "Knock it off."

They separated, and West raised his eyebrows. "What's the matter, Prescott? Are you jealous?"

"Hardly." He was glad Olivia had met her match. That West was taking her for a heartfelt ride. But that didn't mean he wanted to watch them swap spit.

"Kyle came here to talk about Joyce," Olivia said, straightening West's tie.

"Really?" The fed seemed intrigued. "She used to have a thing for me."

Now Kyle was jealous. "She did not." He turned to Olivia. "Did she?"

"She thought he was hot when she first met him. But that was before we hooked up."

"I guess there's no accounting for taste. Not that it matters." He rose from the sofa, ditching the stupid pillow. "I'm not interested in her."

West and Olivia exchanged an oh-sure look.

"I'm not," he reiterated.

Olivia walked him to the door. "You want to sleep with her."

"That's doesn't mean I'm going to."

She shook her head, as if she didn't believe him, as if he didn't have the slightest bit of willpower.

As if a blue-eyed blonde, a cop no less, could bring him to his knees.

The following day, Joyce prepared for the silent war churning inside her. Her personal fight. And the battle she intended to wage against Kyle. There was more than one way to skin a cat, to strip a tiger down to the bone. This time, she was going to dupe him.

She glanced around, surprised by what she saw. His basement had been converted into a gym, and unlike the rest of his house, the room was spotless. Every piece of machinery gleamed.

Finally she met his gaze. He stood across from her on a sparring mat. He wasn't armed. No holster. No semiautomatic weapon. He wore standard gray sweatpants and a ribbed tank top.

He looked dangerous, tall and strong and strapped with muscle. His hair was secured in the usual manner, with a cotton cloth tied around his head.

He moved closer, and she withheld a triumphant smile. He couldn't keep his eyes off her cleavage, off her scooped neckline.

"You're staring," she said.

"Because that's not proper attire."

"These pants are made for working out. Lycra stretches."

"I was talking about that skimpy top," he said, even though her skintight capris had caught his attention, too.

"I didn't know there was a dress code. Besides, I'm wearing a push-up bra."

His gaze drifted again. "I noticed."

"I wore it for you. For your fantasy."

"Don't mess with me, Joyce."

"Is that what I'm doing?" She batted her lashes, poking fun at their attraction.

He rolled his eyes, and she laughed, breaking the tension, the male-female heat that crackled in the air.

But she was just getting started, letting him think she wasn't a threat. That she wasn't clever enough to outsmart him.

"Good thing I didn't wear spiked heels," she told him. "Or no panties."

He merely blinked.

"Are you ready?" she asked.

He didn't answer.

"Kyle?" she pressed.

"Of course I'm ready." He copped a macho stance, widening his legs and planting his feet in a solid position. "I'm not going to fall for your little game."

She glanced at his tank top. His nipples were erect. Hers were, too. They protruded like .45 caliber bullets, jutting against the silky fabric of her bra. A condition that didn't go unnoticed.

He was already falling for her game.

She tucked her hair behind her ears and told herself there was no such thing as a dumb blonde. Women who used their sexuality knew exactly what they were doing.

Not that she was going to seduce him. The idea was to set him up, to divert his attention. The way he'd done to her when he'd faked that kiss.

The session began, with Kyle pointing out the mistakes she'd made yesterday, explaining why her moves hadn't been effective on him. According to him, she'd been trained properly in the past, but she wasn't using her knowledge to her best advantage.

She stepped back and watched him demonstrate his style, his techniques. He reminded her of Tarzan. Fluid, natural. A man who'd been born to bend his body, to kick, to spin, to conquer the jungle.

When they began sparring, she went after his vulnerable areas. He blocked her, of course. He wasn't going to let her crush his Adam's apple or knee his kidneys. But he commended her anyway.

For a moment, she wondered if she should cut her losses and forget about the way he'd tricked her. But then she caught him looking down her top, stealing peeks between all those muscular moves.

Tarzan was getting turned on.

They kept sparring, making physical contact. She worked hard, concentrating on the lesson. She listened to his instructions. She followed his advice.

He was a damn good instructor. But that didn't mean she was going to let him win.

By the time they took a break, her skin was damp and warm.

He walked over to a minifridge in the corner, removed two bottles of water and handed her one.

"Thanks." She sipped, and he guzzled, like the Cro-Magnon he was. She wasn't buying his story that his predecessors didn't drag women off by their hair.

He wasn't swigging from thirst. He hadn't even broken a sweat. If anything, he was trying to temper his overactive libido.

Time to go for the gold, she thought. To get her revenge. With as much drama as she could muster, she poured some water down her top, letting it trail between her breasts.

He gaped at her. "What are you doing?"

"Cooling off."

"This isn't a wet T-shirt contest."

"I'd have to take my bra off for that."

"You better not."

She almost laughed. He was angry. Ticked that she was toying with him. Big, primordial ape.

He moved closer. "Cut the crap, Joyce."

"I'm just having a little fun."

"And I already told you that I wasn't going to fall for your game."

She glanced at his groin. She wanted to give him a swift kick, but she knew he was wearing a cup. Men like Kyle didn't spar without protection.

She tugged at her water-misted top. "Maybe I will take off my bra. It's starting to itch."

"Do whatever you want. It's not going to make a difference."

Oh, yes it would. She reached back and unfastened the hooks. But as she maneuvered the garment under her top, she pretended that she was having trouble. That she couldn't get the straps down.

He chuckled under his breath. And better yet, he moved even closer, letting down his guard.

"You're a hell of a seductress, Detective."

She played up her dilemma, giving him a slapstick show. She kept flailing her arms. He was too tall to punch in the nose, so she raised her fist and surprised him with an uppercut, catching his jaw, hitting him as hard as she could.

Score one for the cop. His head snapped on his neck.

Her big bad trainer wasn't chuckling anymore.

"Damn." He rubbed his chin, scraping his hand across the surface of his skin. "You got me good."

She took his unexpected compliment to heart. Her knuckles throbbed like crazy, but it was worth it. "Thanks."

"Want to smack me again?"

While he was primed and ready? Fat chance of that. "That's okay. We can just call it even."

"Like hell we can." He locked his foot around her ankle and tripped her. No fancy moves. No spins, no kicks. Just a smart-aleck trip.

She landed on the mat with a thud. He laughed, and

she grabbed his leg and pulled him down, too. They attacked each other, wrestling like a couple of kids.

The horseplay continued, back and forth. She yanked on his headband and tried to blindfold him with it. He faked a blow to her chin, teasing her for socking him in the jaw.

Then he rolled on top of her. Two hundred pounds of testosterone. Within an instant, her body was pinned beneath his, a lot like yesterday. "You're on a power trip, Prescott."

He smiled. "You think?"

"Yeah, I do." She noticed he gave her more rein this time, enough to fight back if she wanted to.

Suddenly he stopped smiling. "You're even prettier up close."

Her heart zapped her chest, a lightning effect that charged her like Frankenstein's monster. She flinched, warning herself to be careful.

His voice turned rough. "I don't like it any more than you do."

"Me being pretty?" She cursed the ragged feeling, the fire-hazard risk. "Actually I'm okay with it."

"I was talking about you and me." His gaze stormed hers, as fierce as a silent war cry, as the ghost of a warrior howling in the wind. "I hate being attracted to you."

She struggled to contain her emotions, to stop herself from shoving her tongue down his throat, from tasting every inch of him. "Then get off me."

"I don't want to." He traced her top, running his fingers along the neckline. Finally he moved lower, untangling the twisted straps of her bra, where they were falling down her shoulders. "And you don't want me to, either."

She'd forgotten about her unhooked bra, about being half-naked under her shirt. No wonder she looked pretty to him. "Maybe I should force you off of me."

"Maybe you should," he told her, without the slightest trace of malice. He was still touching her, still righting her mangled clothes, respecting her in a way she'd never imagined.

Like a heart-pounding fool, she let him stay there, body to body, breath to breath. But even so, she fought the urge to put her arms around him, to hold him. She'd known him for eight months, almost long enough to have a baby.

That alone scared the death out of her.

Her biological clock wouldn't quit ticking.

"We're in trouble," he said.

Joyce didn't argue. She looked into his eyes, knowing he was going to kiss her.

As softly as they both could endure.

Three

Kyle studied Joyce's expression. She was waiting for his lips to touch hers, for the confusing tenderness they both craved.

He smoothed a strand of her hair. She looked delicate, vulnerable, so unlike the tough-girl cop he knew her to be.

His willpower sucked, he thought, as he lowered his head and closed his eyes.

Their mouths met, and the flavor swirled in his mind. He tasted lipstick and spearmint, a combination that made his head spin.

She ran her hands along his spine. A touch so light, so tentative, he barely knew it was happening.

Wanting more, he used his tongue, taking the kiss to the next level.

She reciprocated, making pleasured sounds. Then she lifted the hem of his tank top and rolled it up a little, just enough to create a shiver.

Fingertips and bare flesh.

He wanted to lift her shirt, too.

Anxious, he positioned himself between her legs, then cursed the metal cup he was wearing, the barrier that kept him from straddling her, from rubbing his body against hers.

He pulled back and opened his eyes.

Silent, she gazed at him, as well.

There she was, all soft and blonde, with her bra still undone and her top slightly skewed. Earlier, he'd tried to fix her clothes and now he wanted to peel them right off. Along with his tank, his sweatpants and the jockstrap that had brought him to his senses.

"You don't have to stop," she said.

"Yes, I do."

"It was just a kiss."

"It was more than that." It was foreplay, he thought. An explosion just waiting to happen. "I don't do this kind of thing. Not with—" He stalled and got to his feet.

"Not with what?" She sat up and struggled to hook her bra. But she was careful not to lift her top, at least not in front.

Kyle thought her cautious manner made her seem vulnerable again.

"Not with what?" she repeated, frowning at him. She still hadn't fastened her bra.

"With women like you," he admitted. "I don't get involved with white women."

Her jaw all but dropped. "That's what this is about? My race? The color of my skin?"

He didn't know how to respond, how to explain why it mattered. She was looking at him as if he were some sort of monster. "I've never been drawn to white women. You're the first one I've ever kissed. Or ever wanted to sleep with."

She ignored her bra and stood up. When she did, the straps peeked out from under her top, falling down her shoulders, the way they'd done earlier. "And that's why you hate being attracted to me? Do you know how offensive that is?"

"It doesn't help that you're a cop."

"Screw you, Kyle. On both counts."

He wanted to move closer, to touch her, to stop her from being so angry, but he kept his hands to himself. "You're making a bigger deal out of this than it is."

"Am I?" She rounded on him. "You're part white. So what does that say about you?"

He wasn't about to answer her question. He didn't want to discuss his childhood with her. Or his adulthood, for that matter. Being a half-blood wasn't easy, not then and not now. "Drop it, Joyce. Let it go."

"Why? Because you don't want to admit that you're a bigot? Do you know how many hate crimes are committed in this country? People bashing other people because—"

"I'm not committing a hate crime. I'm not hurting anyone." As soon as those words spilled out of his mouth, he wanted to take them back. He'd just hurt her. He could see it in her eyes.

Blue eyes. White eyes, as his ancestors used to say.

"Why do you hate being attracted to me?" he asked, turning the tables on her.

"Not because you're Apache. I don't let someone's race get in the way."

"Then what is it?"

"I'm not sure. Maybe it's the way you make me feel. All hot and jumbled. Not like myself."

"You do that to me, too."

"I know." She grabbed her gym bag. "But I'm not interested in training with you anymore."

"So that's it? We're done?" He shouldn't care. It shouldn't matter. But it did. The thought of losing her clenched his gut. He didn't want her to disappear.

Yet when she left, when she walked away, he let her go, unable to admit that the choice he'd made was based on prejudice.

* * *

At 9:00 p.m. Kyle walked through the courtyard of Joyce's apartment building. She lived in a large complex, with flourishing flower beds, lush green-belts and winding hardscape.

He approached the sidewalk that led to her stair-well and frowned at the path in front of him. He'd called Olivia and asked her for Joyce's address, and now he was taking reluctant steps to her door.

He'd never apologized to a woman before and the notion of saying "I'm sorry" was making him squeamish. He'd rather be tortured, stretched on a medieval rack with metal thumbscrews on his hands and an iron mask on his face.

Then what was he doing here?

He ignored the question and started up the stairs. Her unit, D-2, was on the right. On the left was D-4. Both doors displayed Halloween decorations. Joyce had chosen a glow-in-the-dark skeleton, a friendly looking fellow who mocked him with a toothy grin.

He knocked on D-2 and waited for her to answer. She didn't respond. So he knocked again, harder this time. He knew she was home. He'd seen her car in the parking structure and if he listened close enough, he could hear strains of one of those crime scene in-vestigation shows on her TV.

As if she didn't get enough of that in real life.

Finally footsteps sounded. But she didn't open

the door. He assumed she was peering through the peephole to see who was standing on her second-story stoop.

He made a face, letting her know that he felt like a fool, keeping company with a plastic skeleton. Lucky for him, the Halloween decoration wasn't obstructing her view.

Or maybe it was unlucky. She still didn't answer.

"Come on, Joyce. Let me in."

Nothing. *Nada.*

"I didn't even bring a gun." He stepped back and turned in a small circle.

Still nothing.

He cursed and removed the skeleton. "Check this out." He waltzed with the bony creature, making its legs dangle. "I bet you didn't know I could dance."

Suddenly a door opened. But it wasn't Joyce. Still romancing the skeleton, he turned around and made eye contact with her neighbors, an elderly couple staring at him as if he'd lost his mind.

"Evening," he said, switching to a tango and dipping the neon bag of bones.

They continued gaping at him. The old man was as bald as a billiard ball and his wife had a neck like a turkey. Kyle figured they'd been married for at least a hundred years.

"What are you doing?" the man finally asked.

"Trying to make Detective Riggs swoon." He used

the skeleton's hand to gesture to his loose-fitting shirt, snug jeans and battered moccasins. "Can't you tell? I'm a regular Romeo."

"He's crazy," the woman murmured.

"I'll bet he's an undercover cop." The husband gave his six-foot-four frame a serious gander. "He's just the type."

Without another word, they closed the door in his face, assuming he was one of Joyce's offbeat peers. Kyle didn't know whether to laugh or defend his own pathetic honor.

"I see you met Mr. and Mrs. Winkler."

He spun around. Joyce had managed to open her door without him knowing it. So much for his warrior skills. She was holding a pistol on him, too.

Him and the skeleton.

"What's going on?" he asked.

"As if you don't know." She closed her door and came outside, instructing him to assume the frisk position.

He couldn't help but grin. "Is this a sexual thing?"

"Don't get cute."

"Yes, ma'am." He decided it might be fun to let a lady cop pat him down. He hung the skeleton back on its nail, spread his legs and pressed his palms against her door. The only problem was that he'd lied about not being armed. He had his favorite SIG shoved in the waistband of his pants, aimed at the family jewels and covered by his shirt.

Good thing the safety was on.

She searched him, getting familiar in all the right places. "Just what I figured." She confiscated the semiautomatic, grazing his abdomen in the process. "Where's your CCW license, Kyle?"

"I don't have one." He'd never bothered to apply for a permit to carry a concealed weapon. Mostly because he knew he'd never get one. California was stingy that way. He turned around, his stomach muscles jumping. Her hands on his body had felt damn good. "Are you going to bust me?"

She motioned with the barrel of his gun. She'd already holstered hers. "Get inside."

He entered her apartment, wondering if she liked cartoons. Quick Draw McGraw had been one of his favorites when he was a kid.

She followed him into the living room, closed the door and removed the magazine from his weapon. Then she retrieved a metal pistol box, put his unloaded SIG inside and locked it. Only then, did she return his now useless gun.

He frowned at her. She hadn't given him the key. Or the magazine. He set the locked box on a nearby table. "I ought to file a complaint against you. Illegal search and seizure. Or sexual harassment or something."

Her smile was brief. Faint. Barely there. By now, she'd stored her pistol, too, keeping it away from him. "You do have nice abs."

"Oh, yeah?" He moved closer, attempting to touch her hair. As much as he hated to admit it, the pale yellow color fascinated him. "So it *was* a sexual thing."

She stepped out of range. "You wish." Her TV played in the background. "What are you doing here?"

"Aside from annoying your neighbors and getting felt up by you? I came to—" he paused to wince "—apologize."

"And I can see that it hurts."

"Groveling is hard for me."

"Then you should do it more often."

"I'm sorry." This time, he managed to get close enough to reach her hair, to let it slide through his fingers. "I'm not a bigot, Joyce. I swear, I'm not."

"Then what are you?" she asked, snaring his gaze, challenging him to delve into his soul.

"A mixed-up mixed-blood, I guess."

After that, he quit touching her. He dropped his hand, trying to look more casual than he felt.

She waited for him to continue. "Aren't you going to tell me why you're mixed up?"

While she was staring at him? Hanging on his every word? "Maybe later." He broke eye contact and glanced around her apartment.

He noticed that she favored dark woods and feminine colors. Her floral-printed sofa reminded him of rainbow sherbet, and the ceramic bowl on her mahogany coffee table was mint green. Just as he'd suspected, she didn't have any living plants, nothing to water or fuss over. The flowers on her dinette set were silk.

He opened the sliding glass door in the living room and walked onto her balcony. It was nothing more than a slab of concrete, but she'd dressed it up with a café table. He envisioned her drinking coffee there, stealing a few quiet moments before she left for work each morning, the calm before the storm that made up her day.

Her footsteps sounded behind him. "What are you doing, Kyle?"

"Analyzing your life." He turned to look at her. She wasn't wearing the same skimpy top she'd had on earlier. The push-up bra was gone, too. She'd donned an oversize T-shirt, tan leggings and thick socks.

"My life?" She leaned against the rail. "You're supposed to be telling me about yours."

"My problem with getting involved with white women?" He knew he owed her an explanation, even if he had to share his jumbled emotions with her. "My parents' relationship influenced me. The interracial difficulties they had."

"Where did you grow up?"

"In New Mexico on the Mescalero Reservation. The Mescalero, Lipan and Chiricahua Apache are there. My mom was Chiricahua, and my father was a teacher on the rez. A white man living out of his element."

She sat at the table. "But he married your mom?"

"She got pregnant with me. It wasn't a match made in Heaven." Kyle didn't sit. He remained standing on the balcony. "They're both dead now."

"I'm sorry."

"I still have family on the rez. Some family in L.A., too. This is where my dad was originally from." He pulled his hand through his hair, removing his headband and stuffing it in his pocket. His hair was thick and dark, like his mom's used to be. "I look like both of my parents. I got his stature and her features. My skin color is somewhere in between. It's obvious to most people that I'm a mixed-blood."

She watched him through soft blue eyes. "You're a handsome man."

"Thanks." He shrugged and pushed the headband farther into his pocket. "Being handsome didn't help when I was growing up. I was part white, and I got a lot of flack for that. Mostly because my dad didn't appreciate Native ways. In those days, a lot of reservation teachers were like that. They were still trying to tame the savages."

"So the other kids took it out on you?"

He nodded. "I did everything I could to seem more Indian, to prove that I wasn't like my dad. All I wanted was to drain the white blood from my veins."

"But you can't, Kyle. It's part of who you are."

"I know. But it only got worse. After my parents got divorced, I stayed on the rez with my mother, and my father went back to L.A. It should have been okay then, but Mom died soon after that." He blew out the breath he was holding. "She was my salvation. The parent who understood me. And then she was gone."

Joyce left her chain and stood next to him, searching his gaze. "What happened? Were you forced to move to L.A. with your dad?"

"He was my legal guardian. He got custody of me after Mom died. And he was bound and determined to teach me to live in his world."

"How old were you?"

"Fourteen." He smiled a little, recalling how rebellious he'd been. "I fought him every step of the way. I became the biggest, baddest urban skin you ever saw."

"Skin?"

"Indian."

"Big and bad." She opened her hands, gesturing to him. "Like the man you are today."

"Pretty much. I got involved in the American Indian Movement. To my dad, that's the worse thing I could have done. AIM was the anti-Christ to him."

"A bunch of hotheaded Natives campaigning for their rights?"

"Exactly. He didn't respect our values, the changes we were trying to make. That's the sort of behavior he'd been trying to tame on the rez. He was backward in that way."

"And it rubbed off on you," she said catching his attention, making him frown.

"My so-called bigotry?"

"You reversed his prejudice. You turned it around to make it work for you."

"I told you I was mixed up."

"You don't have to be. You don't have to avoid non-Native relationships. If you're attracted to someone, it shouldn't matter."

"I know. It shouldn't. But it does. And not just because of my dad. I'm not actively involved in AIM anymore, but I'm part of a Warrior Society, a militant group. I'm a full-force activist, Joyce."

She looked him straight in the eye. "I know who you are."

Of course she did. She was a cop. The lady who'd confiscated his gun. "How would it look for a half-blood who fights Native causes to date non-Native women? Especially white women?"

She heaved an audible sigh. "So you're living by an image? By what's expected of you?"

"Yeah. I guess I am." And the revelation hit him like a fist, hard and deep, right in the solar plexus. "That sucks, doesn't it? The big bad skin worrying about what other people think?"

"It's keeping you out of my bed," she said, walking into the house and leaving him alone on the balcony.

He simply stood there, for at least five minutes, staring after her. What the hell was that? A make-him-suffer rebuff? A slap in the face?

Screw this, he thought. He followed her, catching her in the kitchen, where she was preparing to make a cup of herbal tea. How frigging refined of her.

"Do you want some?" she asked.

"No." He crowded her.

"Back off." She tried to nudge him out of her way.

"Don't act like all of this is my fault. If push came to shove, you wouldn't be seen with a guy like me. Not publicly."

She turned on the stove and the flame ignited, a bit like her temper. "Is that your answer to everything? Blaming other people?"

He ground his teeth. He wanted to grab her and kiss her, shut her up with his tongue. "You're avoiding my accusation."

"This is about sex, Kyle. Neither of us is looking for anything beyond an affair."

How was he supposed to know what she was looking for? Women never made any sense. How many times did they say one thing, then do another? "I thought you weren't interested in banging my brains out. I thought you came to me for training. To fight your way out of your problems, not to fu—"

"Don't talk to me like that." She cut him off before he could get too crude. "It's offensive."

He watched her remove a jar of honey from the cabinet above her head. It bothered him that she was still being pissy. That she hadn't let him off the hook. "Will you go on a date with me?"

She nearly dropped the honey. "What?"

"You heard me."

She pressed the bear-shaped jar against her chest. "When?"

"Tomorrow night. We'll go to a strip club or something."

"Very funny."

"Fine." He refused to smile. "We'll have dinner."

She removed the near-boiling water from the stove and poured it into her cup. She wasn't smiling, either. "Will you wear a suit?"

"Get real." He bumped her arm and made her spill the water.

She rounded on him. "You did that on purpose."

He stood his ground. She knew better than to try to fight him. "Are you going to go out with me or not?"

"I suppose I could."

"Such enthusiasm." He turned to leave. "You better heat some more water."

"Just get out of here."

"Be glad to."

Before he walked out of the kitchen, she stopped him. "What time are you picking me up tomorrow?"

"Seven."

She refilled the pot. "Don't be late."

"You, either." He went into the living room and wondered what he'd just gotten himself into.

He reached for the metal box with his SIG and decided to pick the lock. While Joyce made tea, he poked around for a paperclip on her rolltop desk, found one and opened the box. Then he located the magazine, loaded the gun and shoved it in the waistband of his pants.

"I'm leaving," he called out to her, deciding she would think twice about disarming him again.

Four

Joyce sat across from Kyle in a restaurant in Universal Studios CityWalk. It wasn't a quiet eatery, considering it boasted three mechanical bulls, three full bars, an outdoor dance floor and stage, live music, karaoke, video monitors and diagonal big screens.

He'd taken her to a tourist attraction for their date.

"Interesting choice," she said.

"We can't avoid the public here."

No kidding. The steak house was centrally located between the entrance of CityWalk and a Universal Studios tour bus parking lot, where the foot traffic was horrendous.

Kyle gestured to a nearby bull. Wooden tables, including theirs, surrounded the pen that housed it. "Want to go for a ride later?"

"Not on your life."

"They give women easy rides." He leaned forward. "Slow and sexy."

She ignored the chill that sleeked up her spine. "With all these people watching. No way."

"I'll do it if you will."

She wasn't about to fall for his bait, to let him talk her into it. "You'd probably kick butt. It's probably right up your alley."

"I'm always up for trying something new."

She raised her eyebrows. "Like dating me?"

"You're my worst nightmare." He flashed a naughty smile. "But damn if you don't look hot."

"Thanks." She wore a slim black dress and classic pumps. "Can you imagine me on the bull in this?"

"Yeah, I can." He took a swig of his beer and settled his gaze on her décolleté. "I totally can."

She fussed with the gold chain around her neck. He was looking at her as if he wanted her to ride him instead. But what did she expect? She'd made good use of the push-up bra, something that was bound to capture his attention.

The waitress brought their meals, and Joyce told herself to relax. She tracked serial killers for a living. Having dinner with Kyle was no big deal.

Then why wouldn't her heart quit pounding?

He was dressed in jeans and a button-down shirt. His jacket was leather. She imagined that was as formal as he got. As for his hair, he'd pulled it into a ponytail, leaving the hard, handsome angles of his face unframed.

She glanced at their plates. She'd ordered a center cut of New York, and Kyle had gone for a twenty-two ounce porterhouse, the biggest steak on the menu. He assaulted it the way he attacked the world. He liked his meat blood red, but that didn't surprise her.

She shifted her gaze, studying his fingers, the way he held his fork. "How did you pick that lock?"

He looked up. "What lock? Oh, you mean the pistol box at your house?"

"The very one." She knew he hadn't found the key. She'd secured that in her pocket.

"I used a paper clip."

She clamped her jaw before it fell. "I paid eighty bucks for that case."

"Then you got ripped off. Either that or I'm a damn good thief."

"What about tonight?" It was impossible to tell what he had going on under his jacket. "Are you armed?"

"No, but if you want proof, you can pat me down. I wouldn't mind a repeat performance."

"I'll bet." She wielded her knife. Her heart was still

pounding, still thumping in her chest. Finally she cut into her steak. It was well-done, the opposite of his.

"Do you think your fellow officers will think you've gone native?" he asked. "Or aren't you going to tell them you're seeing me?"

"I haven't decided." Going native meant police burnout, a cop suffering a mental breakdown, drinking too much, doing drugs, carousing. "Clever play on words." In this case, going native meant keeping company with a lust-driven Apache.

They both fell silent, and she wondered if he was going to tell his Indian comrades about her. Somehow, she envisioned him keeping quiet.

"This is a good start," she said. "I'm glad you brought me here."

His gaze drilled hers. "Are you?"

"Yes. This place is perfect." It was loud and raunchy, but the tourists made it seem normal. They were regular people, not L.A. hipsters.

Proving Joyce's point, a fifty-something woman in polyester pants and a lightweight sweater climbed onto the mechanical bull. Her ride was slow, but far from sexy. Yet that hardly mattered. Her family was cheering her on.

Kyle watched the activity. "Looks like they're having fun."

"Yes, it does." She felt a pang of familiarity. The woman's husband was giving her pointers, and the people Joyce assumed were her children were young adults, probably with chaotic lives of their own, but the bond was there, the undeniable connection. "My family is like that."

"Your mom would come here and ride a bull?"

That made her laugh. Her mother was an old-fashioned, sweetly behaved homemaker. "No. But she's our foundation. She holds all of us together."

"All of you?" He sat back and examined her. "Do you come from a big family?"

"Six girls."

"Damn. I'll bet your dad went crazy. All that hairspray and perfume in one house." He made a face. "Not to mention PMS six times a month." He paused, pondering the situation. "Seven if you include your mom."

Joyce shook her head. Kyle never failed to express his chauvinist views. She balled up an extra napkin and threw it at him. He shrugged and tossed it back at her.

The woman's ride ended. She walked over to her family, where good cheer erupted. Her husband gave her a playful swat on the bottom.

The pang of familiarity returned. Joyce's dad did that to her mom, too. "My father is a retired police officer."

Kyle frowned a little. "Is he the one who influenced you?"

"I always loved hearing about his job." To her, it

had seemed far more exciting than her mom's station in life. But now she didn't know what to think. Those baby urges were messing with her brain.

"Are any of your sisters cops?"

"No." They all had a career of some kind, and they all had husbands and kids, but no one, not even their husbands were in law enforcement. "They worry about me the way they used to worry about Dad."

"That's understandable. It's human nature, I guess. We live in violent times."

She gave him a pointed look. "With men who carry guns. Men who aren't supposed to."

He came forward in his chair. "Then your sisters have a lot to worry about, don't they?"

"I should have busted you."

He smiled. "Yeah, but you went out with me instead." He saluted her with his empty beer. "The girl's got guts."

She smiled, too. "Or mush for brains."

They finished dinner, and he insisted on dessert. Not that Joyce was opposed to a hunk of chocolate cake. She just imagined it going to her hips. Still, it didn't take much to persuade her.

"Do you want to dance later?" he asked. "The band comes on around eleven."

She dived into her cake, knowing she would have to hit the gym first thing in the morning. "Dance?"

"Did you think I was goofing around with the skeleton? Those were some serious moves."

She bit back a smile, recalling the way her neighbors had gaped at him. "Very serious. Debonair, too."

"Damn straight."

She glanced at her watch. Eleven o'clock was still an hour away. "What should we do in the meantime?" Her dessert was nearly gone. His, too. He'd practically inhaled it. But he probably worked out for at least four hours a day, loving every excruciating minute of it. For that, she wanted to kick him.

"We could browse around like everyone else," he said.

"Are you suggesting that we behave like tourists?"

"Why not? There's a slew of specialty stores. There's even a gothic shop. An entire building filled with creepy collectibles."

"Just what every homicide detective needs. More gore." She ate the last of her cake and decided that being a tourist sounded fun. She couldn't remember the last time she'd shopped in nonsensical stores. And never with a man like Kyle.

To Kyle, CityWalk was like Disneyland, Hollywood Boulevard and the set of a blockbuster movie all rolled into one. Where else could you find a crashed flying saucer protruding from the roof of a sci-fi store? Or how about a rock and roll bowling alley? Music madness and retail mayhem, he thought. It didn't get any better than this.

A stroke of marketing genius, CityWalk catered to over eight million people a year. Kyle and Joyce became two in a crowd.

The first store they wandered into was a place that specialized in wind-up toys. Kyle felt like a kid in a pineapple under the sea. He found a SpongeBob Squarepants boat he was dying to have.

He showed it to Joyce. "It drives around in circles."

She angled her head. "So?"

"So, I'm buying it."

"For who?"

"Myself."

She clucked her tongue. "Seriously?"

"Would I lie about my favorite cartoon character?"

"No. I suppose not. My nieces and nephews like him, too. But they're a lot younger than you." She removed the boat from his hand and examined it. "Is this for the tub?"

"Yeah." He moved closer, stealing a perverted peek down the front of her dress. "Want to soak with me later? We can test it out."

She held the wind-up toy between them. "Not without bubble bath."

Was she kidding? He would buy her a gallon of whatever tripped her fancy.

He paid for the boat, then escorted her outside,

where they returned to the shopping walk. He kept his eye open for girly stores, retailers that might sell bath and body products. He had no idea if Joyce was teasing him, but he was willing to take a chance.

He spotted a shop with pretty things in the window. They went inside, and sure enough, there was a collection of bubbly items on a glass display.

"Pick out what you want," he said.

"I never said I wanted anything."

"Humor me," he told her. "Give me a thrill."

She couldn't decide. She looked at everything, fingering all the festive bottles and shrink-wrapped baskets. Finally she chose a bubble bath with an oceanic scent.

Kyle wasn't sure what that meant. "It doesn't smell like saltwater, does it? That might be okay for SpongeBob, but—"

She laughed and popped the cap, waving the bottle under his nose. The fragrance was crisp and sensual, breezy and fresh. It made him want to strip her where she stood.

He took the bubble bath to the front counter and noticed a package of little pots advertised as lip sugar.

He glanced at Joyce. She stood next to him in line, her stretchy black dress capturing her breasts and flowing to her ankles. He decided that lip sugar was just what they needed.

In or out of the tub.

He grabbed the shimmering pots, and she slanted him a curious look. He read the package. "They're flavored. Cranberry, papaya, watermelon and mango. Just imagine what we can do with this stuff."

She leaned against him, pressing her mouth to his ear. "This isn't a sex shop, Kyle."

It might as well have been. He turned his head and kissed her, fast and furious, leaving her breathless when he was done. He didn't care how many people were in the store.

Joyce righted her clothes afterward, smoothing the front of her dress and wobbling on her pointed-toe pumps. Kyle hadn't touched her dress or her shoes. But apparently he'd made her feel sexually skewed.

What could be more perfect than that?

He paid for the items and gave her the bag. She smacked him with it, and they both laughed. He wondered if she'd brought her gun, if it was stuffed in her purse with a classy compact and a pair of police-issued handcuffs.

Lord, he hoped so.

They continued shopping, killing time and driving each other crazy. He bought a Wolf Man doll in the gothic place and made it attack a shelf of Barbie dolls in the regular toy store.

"Stop it." Joyce repositioned the Barbies he'd knocked over. "You're going to get us in trouble."

"We've been in trouble since we met." He removed Wolfy from the box, figuring the hairy guy could have more fun that way. "Did you play with Barbie when you were young?"

"Of course I did." She grabbed Wolf Man, stopping him from destroying another display. "I had her house, her car, the whole bit. So did my sisters."

"What about Ken?"

"What about him?"

"He always seemed like a wuss to me. They should have given her a stud like G.I. Joe." He hunted around for Barbie's latest car and discovered that she had all sorts of vehicles. The Happy Family Volvo fascinated him, so he decided to buy it for Wolf Man.

"This is big enough for Frankenstein and Dracula, too. I have them at home. Just imagine the road trip they can go on."

She looked at him as if he'd gone mad. "Maybe they can tow SpongeBob's boat while they're at it."

"Don't get smart. You and all of your Barbie accessories. Girls get everything."

"And boys like you make girls like me run the other way." She blew out an exaggerated breath. "Olivia told me you were bizarre."

Kyle shrugged. Most women couldn't get past his quirks, but he could tell that Joyce was enjoying his company, even if she thought he was strange. "That's not all Olivia told you."

She shook her head, and he merely gazed at her. There was no point in denying that he'd confirmed what had been discussed. He was the first to admit that he was a sexual egomaniac.

She held Wolf Man like a baby, cradling him against her breast. "What am I going to do with you, Kyle?"

He reached out and touched her cheek. Her skin was the color of honey and cream and candlelit ivory. "You can do whatever you want."

She released a shaky breath. Only this time she wasn't faking it. "Wanting you this badly scares me."

"Sometimes being afraid is good." He kissed her, tasting her fear, her passion, the forbidden urges driving her into his arms.

Their bodies bumped. He was too tall for her, but with heels, she made an erotic fit. He liked the way she felt next to him. Warm and womanly, with her pulse battering his. "Are you ready to dance?"

She nodded. "I'm ready."

They separated, and he took her hand. Damn if he wasn't aroused, if her anxiety didn't excite him.

They walked to the parking lot and put their packages in his SUV, then returned to the restaurant, where the nightlife thrived.

The band played a variety of music, songs that went from slow to fast to somewhere in between. Some riffs were twangy, some were sleek and sensual.

Kyle guided Joyce onto the dance floor and they

found the rhythm. They moved, hip to hip, rocking back and forth. There wasn't a lot of space. Other couples crowded them, forcing them toward the edge of the stage.

Then suddenly she slid her hands inside his jacket.

Talk about getting turned on. "Are you frisking me?"

She went lower. "You told me you wouldn't mind a repeat performance." She grazed the front of his pants, but there was no SIG, no semiautomatic weapon to bust him for. The hardness was him.

He wanted to haul her against his fly, to make damn sure she felt it. He wanted to pull down the front of her dress, too. Right here, right now. His mind was spinning, going in lethal directions. "Maybe you better be careful."

"Me?" She backed him against a wall, where the music vibrated. They weren't on the dance floor anymore. They were in a darkened corner. "I have the law on my side."

"And I'm bigger than you. Stronger." He switched places, pinning her against the wall. "If I go home with you tonight, your badge won't matter." He snared her wrists, holding them above her head. "It won't mean a thing."

She didn't fight him off. But she didn't submit, either. She challenged him instead, looking into his eyes. "Who says I'm letting you come home with me?"

"No one. I'm just giving you fair warning." He released her. "You were afraid earlier."

"And you said that sometimes being afraid can be good."

"It can. As long as it brings out a person's survival skills." He smoothed her hair. "I still don't know what's going on in your life. If you can survive what's happening between us."

She barely blinked. "I already told you that I wasn't looking for anything beyond an affair."

Yeah, she'd told him. Last night. While she'd been on the defense. He wasn't sure if that counted. "What if you're too confused to know what you want?"

"I'm not going to get attached, not to a guy like you." She batted his hand away from her hair. "That's not what scares me."

"Then what is it?"

"Edgy sex. I'm afraid I'll do things to you that I've never done before. That I'll let you do even kinkier stuff to me."

His heart struck his chest. "Really?"

"Really."

"In that case." He grabbed her and kissed her, and when she reacted like a black widow, nearly swallowing him whole, he gave up the fight, dragging her against his body. If she wanted to eat him alive, he would let her.

But he didn't know if she was going to take the

next step, if she would actually invite him to her bed. Kyle didn't take anything for granted.

Especially women.

Five

After their date ended, Kyle and Joyce arrived at her apartment building. He pulled into a guest-parking stall and killed the engine.

Joyce didn't know what to say, what to do. If she asked him to come upstairs with her, it wouldn't be for a nightcap. They were beyond that point.

It was sex or nothing at all.

He turned to look at her, and her pulse went crazy, electrifying every part of her body.

"Have you ever done it in a car?" he asked.

She tried to maintain her composure. She'd never met anyone quite like him. "No. Have you?"

"Are you kidding?" He shot her a teasing grin.

"Me?" He reached over and opened the glove compartment. "Check out the condoms."

Sure enough, there was a variety pack crammed into the tight space. "You're not supposed to store them where they can be exposed to heat. It will damage the latex."

"I know. But I don't keep them here for extended periods of time. I'm careful about that. I replace them as often as I can."

"It's indecent exposure," she said, itching to riffle through the box.

"What is?"

"Having sex in a car."

"That's what makes it so fun."

She gave in and grabbed the condoms. She poked through the box, raising her eyebrows at him when she came across a glow-in-the-dark style.

He shrugged and then laughed. "They're phosphorous."

"Only a man like you would use his penis for a night-light."

He laughed again. "I'm a novelty kind of guy." He moved closer to her, leaning across the center console. "These are my favorite." He removed several packages that had *warm sensations* written on them. "They're lubricated with this stuff that makes both partners feel warm and tingly."

Joyce was already feeling warm and tingly. His

face was only inches from hers. He was close enough to kiss, to taste, to tempt, to tease.

They stared at each other, and then his eyes, his tiger's gaze, made a predator's sweep, moving up and down. She couldn't help it. Her nipples went hard.

"I want you to take off your dress," he said.

So did she. She wanted to strip down to her panties and bra and climb in his lap. But if they got caught, her job would be on the line. Law-abiding detectives didn't have sex in cars, in public places where they could be seen.

He whispered against her ear. "You're thinking about it, aren't you?"

"Yes."

"Then do it."

"I can't."

"Then let me do it."

She shook her head. "You're trying to corrupt me."

"Then tell me to go home. Send me away."

"I can't do that, either." She traced the angles of his face, the sculpted edges, the hollow ridges, the untamed beauty. "I want you to stay."

His lips formed a sensual slant, exposing a flash of teeth. "Now *you're* trying to corrupt *me*."

"I don't think that's possible."

"Yes, it is. You, with your pretty blond hair and cop-girl ways. I shouldn't be with a lady like you."

He glanced at her satin handbag. "Do you have handcuffs in your purse?"

"What? No." She tried to calm the pounding in her chest, the runaway beats of her heart. "I don't bring handcuffs on dates."

"Do you have some in your apartment?"

"Yes."

"Can I lock you up with them?" he asked. "Would you trust me to do that?"

"Is this a trick question?"

"No." He slid his hands through her hair, then put a strand a across her mouth. "No trick."

She gripped his shoulders, and he kissed her, sucking on her tongue and her hair. She closed her eyes, loving every second of what he was doing.

When he let her go, she wanted to crawl all over him. But she was nervous, too. The anxiety of being with him hadn't gone away.

"Are you okay?" he asked.

"I'm fine."

"You don't look fine."

She dropped her hand to her knee, curling her fingers around her dress. She didn't know how to explain her feelings, how to tell him what he did to her. "You overwhelm me, Kyle."

"I can't change who I am." He frowned, then smoothed her hair, taming the strand that had been in his mouth. "I'm crude and hard. I'm not good at being romantic."

"I don't care about hearts and flowers." And his touch was gentler than it should have been, much too tender for a man who claimed to be so hard. "That's the last thing I want."

"Maybe so. But most women like that kind of stuff. Why would you be any different?"

"I just am."

"But why?" He pierced her with a ravening gaze, with a look that was becoming all too familiar. "Because you're a cop? Is that what sets you apart?"

"Yes." That and her determination to stop herself from lusting after a husband, from wanting a baby.

"Then get edgy with me, Detective. Make our cravings worthwhile."

"I will. I am." As a surge of adrenaline spiked her veins, she gave herself permission to enjoy him, to take him upstairs, to keep him.

All night long.

Kyle and Joyce entered her apartment, and when she closed the door, he watched her turn the dead bolt and latch the chain, locking them inside.

He'd brought their packages in from the car. He'd brought the entire box of condoms, too, stuffing them into one of the bags. He intended to have a wicked time with Detective Riggs. He couldn't remember wanting a woman so badly.

She didn't say anything, and neither did he. They stood in the living room with two Tiffany-style lamps burning brightly. The mottled glass shades created a prism of color. They were pretty, but they weren't the real thing. Kyle had a hundred year old Tiffany lamp in storage that would probably blow her away. He wondered if she would think he was crazy if he gave it to her.

She clutched her handbag, and he noticed the simple gold clasp. Was she being honest about the hearts-and-flowers thing? Maybe. And maybe not. She still had some issues in her life that she refused to talk about.

"Is sex going to help?" he asked.

She set her purse down. "With what?"

"Your problems."

She managed a risqué smile. "I hope so."

"More than sparring with me? More than our training sessions?"

"I can't spar with you in bed?"

Now it was his turn to smile. "Does it have to happen in bed?" He gestured to her flowery sofa, to the dining room table, to a chair that would probably collapse with their combined weight. "We could attack the rest of your furniture. Or the floor. Or maybe the concrete on the balcony." He watched her eyes go wide. "I'm not picky."

"I want you in bed." She took his arm and led him down the hall.

He didn't complain. He liked being a willing captive. Besides, he took one look around her room and got even more turned on. It was soft and feminine, with a white quilt and lacy sheers. She even had a vanity table with a gilded mirror and perfume bottles on the marble top. A 9mm Glock rested on the vanity, too.

Before he could draw his next breath, she tossed handcuffs onto the bed. Kyle nearly fell to his knees. The double-locking device was even sexier than her gun.

He emptied their shopping bags, where the condoms, lip sugar and bubble bath tumbled onto the quilt. The toys fell out, too.

Suddenly they both laughed.

And then they stared at each other.

"Will you take your dress off for me?" he asked.

She nodded and reached for the zipper. He watched and waited, his skin going warm. The metal teeth made a sliding sound.

Finally she dropped the dress and stepped out of it. She wore a black push-up bra, matching panties and thigh-high hose, the modern kind without garters. The tops were banded in lace, where they stayed up on their own.

"You're beautiful," he told her.

She closed her eyes, held them tightly shut, then opened them. "That sounded romantic."

Damn. "It did?"

"Yes."

"Sorry." He righted the compliment. "You look like one of those girls who jump out of cakes."

She adjusted her bra, exposing more cleavage. "That's better."

He walked over to her. In spite of her bravado, he could tell she was nervous. Earlier, he'd reminded her that he was bigger and stronger. That her badge wouldn't matter. Yet she'd offered him her handcuffs anyway.

Was she regretting her decision?

"I won't hurt you, Joyce."

"I trust you."

"No, you don't. Not completely." But he wanted her to enjoy the experience, to have fun, to let her inhibitions go. "We don't have to do anything that makes you uncomfortable."

"I know, but…"

"But what?"

"Edgy sex scares me." She fussed with her bra again. By now the tops of her areolas were exposed, and her legs were slightly parted, her stance long and lean. "Yet I'm willing to chance it. At least with you."

He wanted to tell her that she was even more beautiful than before, but not at the risk of sounding romantic. "The parts of our brain that control fear, anxiety and arousal are close together." He kept his gaze locked onto hers. "So close that a little bit of nervousness can enhance the pleasure."

"When are you going to do it?"

He knew she was talking about the handcuffs. "Later."

"How much later?"

"After we're both naked." He removed his boots, then bared himself to the waist, leaving his jeans intact. For now, he wanted to focus on her.

Anxious, he moved forward, reached around, unhooked her bra and got rid of it. Her breasts spilled into his hands. She made a sweet sound, and he thumbed her nipples. Pink and pearled, they stood out against the whiteness of her skin. She was so different from him, so soft and fair.

Fascinated, he went lower, moving to her stomach. She had an athletic body, perfect for a man's greedy touch. Next he toyed with the waistband of her panties. She quivered, and he slipped his hand inside, then used two fingers, plunging deep.

Quick and hard.

He barely gave her time to think. She gasped, and he smiled. "Surprise attack."

She gripped his shoulders. "You're good at that."

"Glad you think so." Kyle pulled her panties down, and her knees nearly buckled. He caught her before she fell, stumbling to the bed, taking her with him.

He pushed the toys, bubble bath, condoms and handcuffs to the edge of the mattress, leaving the flavored gloss at his disposable.

He opened the shimmering pots, then handed her the watermelon flavor. "Are you ready to play, Detective?"

Her voice vibrated. "Yes."

"Then be bad for me," he said, challenging her to take control, to lead them both into temptation. "As naughty as you can get."

Joyce couldn't believe what she was doing. Messing around with a man she barely knew. Getting caught up in sinful games, in the thrill of dangerous sex.

She took the gloss and painted it around her belly button, then drew a line downward, stopping before she reached her pubis.

"Do it there," he said.

Her pulse skipped. She wasn't ready. She needed more time. More courage. "Not yet."

She put a dollop inside her navel, then went in the other direction, dabbing the gloss onto her nipples, moving in tiny circles, encouraging him to follow her path.

He did, every step of the way. He licked; he sucked; he sent erotic chills up and down her spine.

When he lifted his head, they kissed, slick and sweet and carnal. And then they rolled over the bed, knocking the condom box onto the floor. She could see the colorful packets spill onto the carpet, scattering like a pirate's treasure. The toys and bubble bath fell onto the floor, too.

Somewhere in the back of her mind, the handcuffs clanked, reminding her of what was yet to come. She'd left both sets of keys on the nightstand, where they remained at Kyle's disposal.

Was she crazy?

Sexually insane?

Her heartbeat staggered, and he pushed another container of gloss into her palm, closing her fingers around it.

"I don't want to wait anymore," he said. "Put this between your legs. Make me taste it."

Heaven help her. She sat up and looked at him. He was looking at her, too. Suddenly she felt like the most desirable woman in the world. He overflowed with lust. She glanced down, shifting the gloss in her hand. "Mango."

His voice turned rough. "Lip sugar."

Much too aroused, she opened her thighs and smeared the sticky cosmetic between her legs. And like the seductress she'd become, she still wore the lace-topped hose and black high heels.

He watched her, and she realized she was touching herself for him. But she didn't care. She liked the excitement, the anticipation, the raw, ragged pleasure.

Joyce scooted closer to him, and he lifted her legs onto his shoulders. She closed her eyes, and he made love to her with his mouth. Deep and dark and hungry. He was like a tiger feasting on his favorite meal, on the prey he'd captured.

She tugged her hands through his hair and opened her eyes. "Kyle."

He glanced up, and their gazes locked.

The intimacy hit her like a fist. She clenched her body to sustain the impact, the force of climaxing all over him, of thrashing through shuddering waves.

When it was over, when she could breathe again, she touched his face. He was still there, between her thighs, watching her.

"That was incredible," she said.

"For me, too." He lowered her legs from his shoulders and removed her stockings and shoes, making her more comfortable. Then he took her in his arms, holding her close.

She rested her head against his chest, telling herself this wasn't romance. But before things got too cozy, she slid her hand to his fly and unzipped his pants. "Are you as big as Olivia says?"

His eyebrows shot up. "You two talked about—"

"Yep." She tugged at his jeans, pulling them and

his boxers down, just enough to see him. He sprang free, granite-hard and porn-star huge.

She sucked in a staggering breath.

He grinned, and she wrestled with his pants, stripping him down to his birthday suit. And then she grabbed the cranberry gloss and rubbed it onto his skin, stroking him with the shiny sweetness.

He opened his legs, surrendering to her ministrations. "You're going to drive me crazy."

"That's the idea." She went down on him, using her tongue, flicking it over the tip.

He shivered, and she settled between his thighs. She couldn't take all of him, but she took as much as she could, making every inch count.

He lifted his hips, getting more and more aroused.

She was excited, too. Thrilled to please him, to suck and nuzzle and make him moan. In the past, she'd found fellatio tedious, something she'd done out of obligation. But with Kyle, it seemed hot and sexy.

She liked the shape of him, the silky hardness, the masculine girth. She even like the way he tasted, the earthy flavor, the primal saltiness.

Giving was as good as receiving.

When he cursed and fisted the sheets, she stopped to gulp some air. "Should I keep going?"

"Yes. No. Damn you." He dragged her up and crushed her mouth with his. The kiss was desperate, rough and insatiable, tongues mating, teeth clashing.

Beneath her hands, his muscles hardened like steel. She traced his abs, enthralled by his nakedness, by the power of how she'd made him feel.

But in the heat of the moment, he stole her victory, proving how big and strong he really was. He grabbed the handcuffs, and her world turned upside down. He didn't chain her to the headboard. He didn't attach her to an inanimate object.

He locked her to him instead, binding their wrists, making them both prisoners.

The lady cop and her lover.

Six

Joyce's heart thundered with every beat. Kyle rolled on top of her with a wicked smile on his face. The handcuffs rattled between them, where his right hand was shackled to her left.

"You tricked me," she said.

"No, I didn't. This is what I had in mind all along."

"Then you should have told me."

"And spoil the fun? Besides, this is perfect for our first time."

She took a labored breath. He made them sound like virgins. "You've never done this before?"

"I've used handcuffs, but I've never attached myself to someone else."

Great. Just great. She couldn't escape his charm. Literally and figuratively.

And that was scarier than what she'd imagined him doing with the handcuffs. In her mind, bondage wasn't nearly this intimate.

"We're going to sleep like this," he said.

"What if I have to get up to go to the bathroom?"

"Then I'll go with you. You're stuck with me, Detective. I already hid the keys."

She glanced at the nightstand. Sure enough, they were gone. He was clever that way: a militant, a magician, a thief.

Kyle snared her gaze, and Joyce shook her head. He was so handsome, so thrilling, so downright domineering, she wanted to knock him on his butt. But she wanted to make hard, hot love with him, too. He was still enormously aroused, his erection pressed against her stomach. She picked up the last pot of gloss—papaya—and waved it under his nose. "We haven't used this one yet."

Aggressive as ever, he took it from her, smeared it all over her lips and pushed his tongue down her throat.

Sultry sex and half-starved sin.

She clawed his shoulders, and they went mad, tumbling over the bed, kissing and biting and battling pheromones.

Within seconds, he went after the condoms on the

floor. Grabbing a fistful, he sorted through them, tossing the rejected packets like confetti.

He tore open a *warm sensation* style, using both of his hands. The motion dragged her chained hand along, too.

"Help me put it on," he said.

She smoothed the latex over him, and he watched her. His stomach muscles jumped, and she realized how anxious he was. His body was taut, waiting for hers. His chest rose and fell.

"You're my captive," she said.

"And you're mine." He nudged her legs apart. "Forbidden lovers."

She lifted her hips. "Dark fantasies."

"Mindless games." He thrust into her, and she caught her breath.

She'd never had anyone as determined, as powerful, as provocative as Kyle. He pumped himself in and out of her, using her for his pleasure.

But she used him, too. She took everything he gave, every low, primal groan, every passionate demand. She met him, stroke for stroke, letting him fill the void, the need that clawed at her soul.

He slid his hand between their bodies and touched her, rubbing and teasing, intensifying the heat, the undeniable wetness. He used the hand that was bound to hers, making her part of his ploy. Suddenly she was touching herself, too, the cold steel grazing her skin.

"I like it when you do that," he said.

"I can tell." His eyes, that catlike gaze, had gone hazy. She was hypnotizing him.

But that didn't stop him from making ruthless love to her. She wrapped her legs around him, grateful for the untamed feeling, for the slick, sliding motion, for the warm, tingling sensation.

"Come for me," he whispered. "Come like you did when I was licking you."

Softly spoken words and a heart-hammering rhythm. She climaxed on command, the naughty sentiment pushing her over the edge.

He kissed her while it happened, and the room started to spin. For her, for him, for both of them. She could feel his need, his hunger, his orgasm threatening to burst.

When it was over, he held her while she quivered beneath him, while she jangled the relentless handcuffs and fell prey to the comfort of his arms.

Kyle nuzzled Joyce's neck. He knew that most women liked to cuddle after sex, so he tried to make it a habit. Of course for him, it was tough to lie still. Cuddling made him want to nibble and kiss and do it all over again.

She shifted in his arms, and he rubbed his cheek against her hair. He liked the feathery softness.

"Don't go to sleep," he told her.

"Why not?"

He bumped his groin against hers. "Because I have to get rid of this condom."

"So get rid of it."

"The trash can is in your bathroom."

She squinted at him. Their faces were just inches apart. "Which means I have to get out of bed, too."

"'Fraid so. You and I are a team."

"You're a pain in the butt, Kyle."

"So are you." He pulled her up, using his chained arm. She made a sour face, and he stole a quick kiss. "But you're a hell of a lay."

"Gee, thanks."

He chuckled and grabbed the bubble bath and toy boat off the floor. "As long as we're in there, we might as well soak in the tub."

She shook the metals cuffs. "In these?"

"Yep. In these. I'm not letting you go until morning."

"Lucky me."

"Don't get snide." He hauled her into the bathroom and discarded the used condom. "I'm the best you'll ever have. You'll never want another guy after me."

"Such ego." She leaned over him while he filled the tub. Then she nibbled his bare shoulder.

He smiled and poured the bubble bath into the water. Having her as a lover was better than he'd imagined.

His first cop. His first Caucasian.

He enjoyed her tough-girl attitude. But he appreciated her dreamy side, too. The lady who'd slipped into his arms after he'd banged her breathless.

"That's enough," she said.

He turned to look at her. "What?"

She grabbed the oceanic liquid from him. "You're not supposed to use the whole bottle."

"Spoilsport." He lowered the boat into the frothing foam. "SpongeBob wanted lots of bubbles."

"You and SpongeBob are weird."

"So are you." He scooped her up, and she squealed like a teenager. He wanted to drop her into the bubbles, but he couldn't, not while they were attached. Holding her was awkward enough. So he climbed into the tub and plopped down, making a dramatic splash and positioning her in front of him.

The tub was too small for both of them, but he didn't care. He opened his legs and bent his knees to make room for her. She leaned back and cozied her butt against him, shifting and moving and driving him to distraction. He moaned, and she laughed.

"You're evil, Detective Riggs."

She wiggled her rear again. "I try."

"No kidding." He wound up the boat, and they watched it drive around in goofy little circles.

He put his free arm around her. "Can you imagine what conjoined twins feel like? Being connected to each other all the time?"

"It's all they know."

"Unless a team of doctors separates them."

She relaxed against him. "I'll bet that's even harder than being together. They probably miss each other afterward."

He rewound the boat when it stopped moving. "Probably."

Her voice turned soft. "Was it lonely for you being an only child?"

The toy bumped his knee, a reminder of his mixed-up youth, of spinning in circles. "Maybe it would have been easier if I had brothers and sisters. They could have suffered with me." He gave the boat a gentle push, away from his knee. "Misery loves company."

When Joyce moved her head, her hair tickled his chest. "Sometimes I used to yearn for privacy, but I wouldn't trade my family for anything."

"Where do you fit in?" he asked. "Are you the oldest? The youngest? Or are you one of the middle kids?"

"I'm the oldest." She heaved a barely audible sigh. "And I used to think I was the wisest. But I don't think so anymore."

"Because of what's going on in your life?"

"I'm my own worst enemy."

He contemplated her response. "You're creating your own turmoil?"

"Yes." She angled her shoulders, turning, trying

to look back at him. Between the cramped quarters and the handcuffs, her mobility was limited. "It's my own fault."

Kyle was as confused as ever, but he didn't expect to understand her. "I've never been able to figure women out. You're such a baffling breed."

She pinched his thigh. "Breed?"

"Gender." He nibbled the side of her neck, tasting soap and skin. "Are you ready to go back to bed?"

"If you are."

"I'm always ready to mess around."

"Oh, I see. Is that why we're going back to bed?"

"Definitely." He stood, giving her no choice but to stand, too. "You can be on top this time."

She nudged him toward the towel rack. "You're such a gentleman."

He knew she was kidding, teasing him for being so blatant, for saying whatever came to mind. He wrapped her in terry cloth, drying her off. He used another towel on himself and dropped both of them onto the floor.

Squeaky clean and warm from the tub, they tumbled into bed. Only this time, they ditched the virgin-white quilt and made use of her pastel-colored sheets.

They didn't bother with foreplay, at least not to the degree of building up the sexual tension. Kyle was already aroused. Just thinking about being with her again made him hard. Joyce seemed just as anxious.

While he leaned against the headboard, she chose a ribbed condom, fitted him with it and climbed onto his lap.

"I like how big you are," she told him, impaling herself with a warm, wet thrust.

Kyle's breath rushed out. "Then go deeper. Take more."

"This much?" She sank onto him again, riding him the way he'd imagined her riding the bull.

"Yeah. That much." He didn't need to lean forward to kiss her. They were already as close as humanly possibly, courtesy of the police-issued handcuffs. "These are better than the sex-shop kind."

She moved up and down, milking every inch. "They're not a toy."

"They are now." He studied her, compelled by her beauty, by the shape of her breasts, the flatness of her stomach, the flare of her hips. He shifted his gaze even lower, mesmerized by the V between her legs.

"You're watching us," she said.

"So are you." He noticed that her head was bent, too.

She kept watching. "It's sexy."

"Totally." Intercourse, he thought. Copulation. The visual effect was driving him half-mad. "Do you like dirty movies?"

She looked up. *"Kyle."*

He stared at her. "Do you?"

She bit down on her bottom lip. "No."

"Liar. You like everything I like."

"No, I don't."

"Yes, you do." He took a chance and whispered something lewd in her ear, something gentlemen didn't say, something ladies shouldn't hear.

She reacted.

Violently.

She called him a bastard, drove her nails into his skin, and then kissed him, nearly devouring his mouth in one fell swoop.

He pushed her down, switching positions so he was on top, so he could pound her into the bed. She wrapped her legs around him, thrashing their shackled wrists.

And then he felt it. The feminine fire. The hot-blooded moisture. The pretty blond cop coming like a call girl.

The edgy sex, the kinky stuff she'd been worried about, was nothing more than a few strategic words. But it didn't matter. Kyle felt as if he'd just scaled a mountain. He loved sex. He always had. But with her, it was even better.

He tugged her head back, using her hair, behaving like the caveman she'd accused him of being. Then he caught himself.

Cursing his stupidity, he released her. "I'm sorry. I wasn't supposed to hurt you."

"Don't apologize." She squeezed her thighs together, tightening her grip, locking him between her legs. "I'm going to hurt you, too."

His heart slammed against his chest. "You are?"

"Without a doubt." This time when she clawed his skin, she drew blood, leaving marks down his chest.

Hard and deep and steeped in pain. They made love like maniacs, and Kyle went off like a six-foot-four rocket.

But he didn't stop when it was over.

He got his second wind and corrupted her, and himself, all over again.

At dawn, Joyce woke up alone. Daylight streamed through the sheers, spilling lavender hues across the bed. She sat up and dragged the sheet against her naked body.

Kyle had left? Just walked out without even saying goodbye? She shouldn't care. But she did.

She glanced at the nightstand. The handcuffs and both sets of keys were there. She peered over the bed and noticed everything that belonged to him was gone, including the confetti of condoms.

He'd taken his protection and hightailed it out of her apartment before she could fix him breakfast or seduce him or kick him out of bed herself.

Damn him anyway.

She stole a panicked glance at the vanity table

just to be sure her gun wasn't missing. Thank goodness. He hadn't disappeared with her Glock.

Joyce slipped on her robe and went into the bathroom. She looked around and noticed that Kyle had tidied up. He'd put the towels he'd dropped on the floor last night in the hamper. Of course, his travel-size toothbrush, which he'd conveniently brought with him, was gone. And so was the SpongeBob boat.

For a man who lived like a slob, he was excruciatingly neat in someone else's home. But that hardly mattered. She would have preferred that he'd said goodbye.

Who cared if—

Suddenly she heard footsteps sounding down the hall. She exited the bathroom, and her heart tripped, just once, before Kyle rounded the corner and nearly bumped into her.

"I was just coming to check on you," he said.

Joyce didn't respond. There he was, half dressed with his hair loose and his ruggedly square jaw in need of a shave.

Finally she found her voice. "Where are the rest of your clothes?"

He made a face at her. "In the closet."

"What about the toy car and Wolf Man?"

"They're in the living room. I was playing with them."

She refused to soften her emotions, to imagine

him pushing around Barbie's Volvo with a werewolf behind the wheel. The man was too damn weird for his own good. "Where are the condoms, the boat and your toothbrush?"

"In there." He gestured to the bathroom.

"They are not."

"Yes, they are. I put everything in the cabinet under the sink. I didn't want you yelling at me for leaving my stuff sitting around."

"You should have told me."

"You were asleep." He made another face. "What's wrong with you? Did you start your period or something?"

She smacked his bare shoulder. He was obsessed with PMS. "No, you big baboon. I thought you ditched me."

A grin crawled across his handsome face. "Before we did it again? Are you kidding? What kind of guy walks out on great sex?" He tugged on her robe. "Are you naked under that ugly thing?"

She glared at him. She wanted to kiss him silly, but she hated to seem too anxious. "My robe isn't ugly."

"Oh, yeah? My grandmother has one just like it."

"Then your grandmother has taste." She tightened the belt on the conservative terry-cloth wrap. "Go make some coffee while I get dressed."

"Only if you promise to have sex with me. Today," he added. "Before I go home."

"We'll see." She turned her back on him and heard him grumble. But he left to brew the coffee anyway.

Joyce brushed her teeth, washed her face and combed her hair, wishing he wasn't so charming.

She climbed into her clothes, wondering if she should make him wait a day or two. Just to prove that she wasn't an easy lay. Of course, that would mean depriving herself, too.

First things first, she decided. Coffee and breakfast.

She entered the kitchen and found Kyle watching the dark liquid brew.

He turned around, and she glanced at his chest. He wasn't wearing a shirt, and his jeans were barely fastened.

He removed two cups from the cabinet and handed her one, making himself at home in her kitchen. "Do you still think I'm a big baboon?"

"No." She poured herself some coffee, adding cream and sugar to it. "I think you're a big, gorgeous baboon."

He laughed and stole a quick kiss. He tasted like mint, like her toothpaste. But so did she.

"What do you want to eat?" she asked. When he shot her a naughty grin, she bit back a smile. "Besides me, you pervert?"

"In that case, you decide."

"Okay, I will." While she opened the refrigerator, he went into the living room and overhauled the toy car, taking it apart and putting it back together.

She shook her head and arranged the ingredients for Spanish omelets and broiled potato wedges.

By the time breakfast was ready, Kyle came to the table with several small toys.

She sat across from him. "What are those?"

"Car seats. This one is for a little kid and this one is an infant seat. The Volvo came with all sorts of accessories." He frowned. "What should I do with them?"

"How should I know?" She didn't want to consider anything that had to do with children, especially newborn babies.

He kept frowning. "Do Ken and Barbie have kids? Or are these for someone else's kids? Barbie's friends or something?"

She cut into her omelet. "I have no idea."

"You should keep track of this stuff."

"Me? What for?"

"You have nieces and nephews."

"That doesn't make me an authority on their toys."

"If I were you, I'd be an authority on their toys."

"Of course you would." She gripped her fork a little tighter. "You're an overgrown ten-year-old."

"There's nothing wrong with being young at heart. Besides, I like kids. I'm good with them."

Joyce gulped her coffee. The last thing she needed was picturing him as the father of her nameless, faceless nonexistent offspring. "If you like children so much, why don't you have any?"

"Because I'm never getting married." He downed the last of his coffee, too. "My mom loved my dad, and he screwed her over. I don't want someone doing that to me. And I don't want to do that to someone else."

"That's understandable." When he set the infant seat on the table, she reached for it. "My parents have been together for nearly forty years. They have an anniversary coming up."

"That's pretty rare these days."

"Yes, it is." She set down the toy, realizing she shouldn't have picked it up to begin with.

"Given your family history, it seems like you would be more marriage minded." He poured ketchup over his potatoes. "But you're not, are you?"

She smoothed her napkin, keeping herself from fussing with the infant seat again. "No, I'm not," she responded, trying to convince herself that she wasn't lying. "My career has always come first."

"I guess that means you're not mom material."

She snared his gaze. "Do I look like mom material?"

"No." He gave her critical study. "But that robe you had on earlier made you look like grandma material."

"So you said." She changed the subject, and they finished their breakfast engaged in another conversation.

Something that had nothing to do with marriage and babies and the hollow ache inside her womb.

Seven

"**A**re you okay?" Kyle asked.

"I'm fine." Joyce ran a sponge across the frying pan she'd used to cook the omelets. She hadn't quit thinking about marriage and babies, and she hated herself for being so weak, so longingly maternal. "I'm rinsing the dishes."

"Looks like you're washing them to me."

She didn't turn around. He was standing behind her, nearly breathing down her neck. "I can't put them in the dishwasher if they have food stuck on them."

"Then what's the point of having a dishwasher?"

"Some models clean better than others. This is a cheap one, I guess." She reached for their plates, and he slipped his arms around her waist. To her, the affection seemed husbandly, and that was a dangerous perception.

Extremely dangerous.

She liked the feeling.

He nuzzled her hair. "What are you thinking about?"

"Nothing."

"You seem preoccupied."

"I'm into the dishes."

"And I'm into you." He sent a ripple of air along her skin. "Really into you."

Water splashed over her hands. She was still rinsing their plates, still trying to control her emotions. He felt so big and strong behind her, so perfectly powerful. The kind of husband a female cop should have. "You just want to have sex."

"Can you blame me?" His voice made her shiver. "We're good together."

Too good. She shut off the faucet, but she didn't turn around. Not yet. For now, she liked being pressed against the sink. Snared. Trapped. At his mercy.

Kyle leaned forward and closed his hands over her breasts, rubbing, making her nipples hard. Then he told her to lift her arms, so he could remove her T-shirt.

She let him undress her. After he discarded her top, he tugged on her sweatpants, pulling them down and helping her step out of them.

Finally she turned around. There she stood in her bra and panties while he still wore his jeans.

Joyce couldn't think of anything to say. Her hands were slightly damp from the dishes, and the sun streamed through the window, bathing Kyle in a warm glow.

He took her in his arms and kissed her.

Softly. Gently.

When they separated, she teetered on her feet. Her brain had zapped back into the husband mode. "Did you bring a condom?" she asked, trying to steer her mind in a safer direction.

"Yes. And I brought this, too." He reached into his pocket and removed a black cloth.

"Your headband?"

"I always have one with me."

"What does that have to do with us?"

He moved closer. "I want to blindfold you."

Her breath rushed out.

"Will you let me?" he asked.

Suddenly he didn't seem like her husband anymore. She glanced at the material in his hand. "Have you done this to other women?"

"Yes."

"Has anyone ever done it to you?"

"You almost did."

Confused, she frowned. Then she recalled teasing him during their first training session, pulling his headband over his eyes while they were rolling around on the sparring mats. But that was before they were lovers. "That doesn't count, Kyle."

"Yes, it does. It turned me on."

She bit back a nervous smile. "Everything turns you on."

He dangled the cloth in front of her. "So can I do it?"

"Where?"

"Here." He pinned her against the sink, the way she'd been trapped before. Only this time, she was facing him. "Right now."

She agreed to play his game, to let him seduce her. "My kitchen will never be the same."

His mouth twisted into a wicked grin. "Every time you wash dishes, you'll think of me. Of this."

He covered her eyes, tying the makeshift blindfold in place, and she became aware of the darkness, of the morning light fading from view. There was nothing but the contact of her lover's hands. A man she was still learning to trust.

"Does it make you feel vulnerable?" he asked.

"Yes. But it feels good, too."

"You like the way I'm touching you?"

She nodded. He roamed her body, molding her as if she were made of clay or wax or a substance she couldn't quite name.

When he reached back and unhooked her bra, her senses heightened, goose bumps peppering her skin. He discarded her panties after that, leaving her naked.

And alone.

He wasn't touching her anymore.

She tried to listen, to decipher what came next. "What are you doing?"

"Looking at you."

Now she felt even more vulnerable. "Whatever you do, don't tell me I'm beautiful."

"But you are. It's not fair that I don't get to say it."

She considered removing the cloth from her eyes and grabbing her clothes. "Being naked and blind-folded isn't beautiful."

"Yes, it is." Before she could end his game, he pulled her tight against him, kissing her hard and fast.

There was no time to let her emotions linger, to give into being self-conscious. She kissed him back, devouring his tongue the way he devoured hers.

He used his fingers between her legs, and she squirmed against the pressure.

"Are you going to take off your jeans?" she asked.

"No."

"Can I take them off of you?"

"No," he responded again.

She gulped the air in her lungs. "Now who's being unfair?"

"Me." He dropped to his knees and put his mouth all over her.

Joyce feared she would lose her mind. She nearly melted on the spot. She couldn't see him. She couldn't watch. But she could feel every warm, spiraling sensation.

She slid her hands through his hair, tangling the thick, straight strands. She wanted more, so much more. By the time it was over, she wanted him inside her.

Dizzy, she leaned against the sink to keep herself steady.

He stood up. She could hear him unzipping his pants and pulling them down. Then the sound of the condom packet being torn open reverberated in her ears. She waited, assuming he was putting on the protection.

What was taking him so long? The seconds seemed like hours.

"I'm too tall for you," he said.

"No, you're not."

"Yes, I am. It will be easier if we—" He stopped talking and lowered her onto the floor, opening her legs to accommodate him.

Finally—*finally*—he entered her, deep and slow. The closeness, the roughness, almost made her weep.

He hadn't removed his clothes, not completely. The texture of his jeans abraded her, but she didn't care. Being blindfolded *was* beautiful, especially when Kyle was inside her.

He made erotic love to her, pushing toward his release. She realized she was on top of her clothes, with her sweatpants cushioning her head.

His climax triggered hers, and for the second time that morning, she burst like a water fountain.

He collapsed on top of her, his body hitting hers with the force of dead weight. But she liked it. She liked the connection.

Maybe too much.

"You're heavy," she said.

He didn't budge. "I am?"

"You know you are." And besides that, he had her arms pinned. She couldn't remove the blindfold. "Come on, Kyle."

"I already did."

"What?"

"Come."

"Very funny." She pushed against him.

A smile sounded in his voice. "That feels good."

"You're insufferable." But she smiled, too.

He stole a quick kiss—something he kept taking the liberty of doing—-and removed the blindfold. She met his gaze, struck by his gold-flecked eyes.

Finally he let her go, lifting his body from hers.

While she sat on the floor and gathered her clothes, he stood up and disposed of the condom, wrapping it in a paper towel and throwing it away in the trash can under the sink. Then he zipped his jeans. She climbed to her feet and got dressed.

"Are you going to get mad if I go home?" he asked.

She adjusted her top and smoothed her hair. "No."

"Are you sure?"

"Yes." In some small way, she *was* angry. Yet in another small way, she wanted him to leave, to quit seducing her.

He shoved the black cloth into his pocket. "I have a training session this afternoon."

"With who?"

"No one you know." He watched her tie the drawstring on her sweatpants. "Are you on vacation for the rest of the week?"

She nodded. "I go back to work next Monday."

"Do you want to come over tomorrow? We can hang out with the dogs or something."

She tried to find an excuse not to drive to the desert, to be with him. "Clyde doesn't like me."

"He'll get used to you." Kyle swooped, pulling her into his arms. "And I want to make the most of what's happening between us."

Her pulse pounded out of control. "What is happening?"

"I don't know, but it's fun. We might as well enjoy it while it lasts."

Yes, she told herself. *While it lasts.* They both knew they wouldn't be sleeping together forever. She took a moment to lean into his embrace, to nuzzle, to kiss. Then she pulled away. "Go home and I'll see you tomorrow."

"Sounds good." He collected his belongings and within no time, he was gone.

The only things he left behind were the toy car seats. Joyce contemplated throwing them away, but she couldn't bring herself to do it.

Instead she tucked them away in a rarely used drawer in her dresser.

Out of sight and out of mind.

Fifteen minutes later, the doorbell sounded. Joyce answered the summons and found her youngest sister, Jessica, on the other side. Accompanying Jessica were her two children. Five-year-old Owen had spiky blond hair, ruddy cheeks and a boyish grin. His baby sister, seven-month-old Gail rested on their mama's hip. Gail, the little gremlin, as Joyce called her, was grinning, too.

"Aunt Joy?" Owen gave her a perplexed look. "How come your Halloween guy looks like that?"

"Like what?"

The child pointed to the door. "Like that."

She poked her head around and saw that Kyle had blindfolded the plastic skeleton before he'd left. Good grief. "One of my friends was goofing around."

"It's funny," the boy said.

"I have funny friends." She lifted the black cloth and changed it to a headband. Owen thought that was amusing, too. A second later, she glanced at her sister. "It's great to see all of you."

"I'm glad you think so. I was worried about intruding on your time off." Jessica transferred Gail into Joyce's arms. "I have to get her playpen. She's been a monster today."

Gail giggled like the gremlin she was. Joyce rubbed her cheek against the baby's hair, her maternal yearnings kicking into high gear.

"Will you watch these two while I go to the car?" Jessica asked.

"Of course I will. But I can help you. We can all go together."

"It'll be easier if I do it alone." Jessica leaned in close. At twenty-six, she hadn't outgrown her long blond hair or her high-school-type rebellions. She hung the diaper bag over Joyce's shoulder. "I'm dying for a cigarette."

"You're supposed to be quitting."

"I know. And that's why I don't want them to see me. Owen will tattle on me. He'll tell his daddy."

Jessica disappeared, and Joyce brought her niece and nephew into the apartment. Owen showed her his latest toy police car. He had a collection of them. He liked officers of the law. He'd been taught they were his friends, and he was old enough to appreciate that Joyce was a cop and that his grandpa used to be one, too.

Joyce sat on the couch, with an overly active Gail on her lap and Owen pushing his black-and-white cruiser around the living room. She thought about Kyle and decided Owen would like him.

When Jessica returned, she barreled into the door-
way. In spite of the playpen she'd lugged up the
stairs, she had a nicotine-satisfied look on her face.

Jessica would probably like Kyle, too. She used
to date bad boys in high school, something that had
disturbed the hell out of their dad.

Luckily she'd married a proper young man. Of
course she had to sneak a smoke now and then. But
her accountant husband adored her.

Jessica opened the playpen and confined Gail.
Then she gave her daughter a bundle of soft, squeaky,
chewy toys. The gremlin amused herself by tossing
them around her cushy cage. Joyce's heartstrings
tugged a bit too hard. She wanted a baby just like
Gail. She wanted a gremlin, too.

Her sister sat beside her on the couch. "Tom was
hoping to set you up with his boss. I know how you
detest blind dates, but he thinks you two would get
along great."

She merely blinked. Tom was Jessica's husband,
and she suspected that his boss was a recently divorced
CPA, probably the man who managed the corporate
accounting firm. "I'm already seeing someone."

"You are?" The younger woman sent her a suspicious glare. "Since when?"

Joyce sighed. She had been dodging her family's
blind date attempts for years. "Yesterday."

"How convenient."

"It's true. We went out last night."

Another suspicious glare. "What's his name and how did you meet him?"

"Kyle Prescott, and he's a friend of a friend."

"What does he do?"

Uh-oh, she thought. Here comes the tricky part. "He's a junk dealer."

"Yeah, right. Now I know you're lying."

"I am not." Joyce looked over at Owen. He was still driving his police car, adding engine noises to go along with it. "That's his main source of income."

"Main source? What else does he do?"

"He teaches close-quarter combat."

Jessica's jaw all but dropped. "That kill-or-be-killed stuff?"

"It's designed to cause permanent damage."

"I'll say. I can't decide if Dad is going to love or hate this guy."

Joyce ignored the glint in her sister's eye. "Dad isn't going to meet him."

"Sure he is. You're going to bring Kyle to Mom and Dad's anniversary party." Jessica scooted to the edge of her seat. "If you don't, I'm going to tell Tom to invite his boss."

"That's blackmail."

"Call it what you will."

"You still don't believe me, do you? You think I'm making Kyle up."

"No, I don't. I think he's the 'funny' friend who blindfolded your skeleton." Jessica lowered her voice. "He is, isn't he?"

Joyce sucked in a breath. "Yes."

"Is he as dangerous as he seems?"

"Of course not," she lied, not wanting to admit to her sister that she was caught up in a thrill-seeking affair. Or worse yet, that every so often, she would envision being married to Kyle. "That was a joke."

"A naughty joke, I'll bet."

Joyce didn't respond. How could she? At this stage, she wondered if she was getting in over her head. If Kyle *was* as dangerous as he seemed.

Eight

The following afternoon, Joyce decided to investigate her lover. She already knew his sexual appetite made him dangerous. But what about the rest of his life? The Warrior Society he belonged to? The Indian activists that kept the authorities guessing?

Needing answers, she shared a scarred wooden table with Special Agent West. He'd agreed to meet her at the Mockingbird, a downtown bar and a cop-patronized watering hole that boasted a jukebox in front and a billiard table in back.

As West nursed a beer, he dipped into a bowl of peanuts. Joyce considered the special agent a friend, and since he was Olivia's boyfriend, he knew Kyle, as well.

At this point, she wanted to talk to the FBI, and West fit the bill. She picked up her drink, a lemon-lime soda, and took a sip. The maraschino cherry had sunk to the bottom of the glass. She could only imagine what Kyle would do with her cherry.

West angled his head, and she frowned. This wasn't the time to be thinking about Kyle's erotic games.

She shifted her attention to the special agent. He wore a black suit, a pale shirt and a narrow tie. His hair was thick and dark, and his eyes were an alarming shade of gray. He was a hell of a profiler, a man who knew what made violent criminals tick.

At the moment, he was analyzing her.

"What's going on?" he asked.

"I want to discuss Kyle with you."

"That's what I figured." He went after another handful of peanuts. "He got you into bed, didn't he?"

"So? Olivia did that to you."

"Yes, but she and I are on the same side. She assists law enforcement agencies." He sat back and gave her an obvious study. "You're worried that Kyle is engaged in illegal activity."

She wasn't about to skirt around the issue, even if Kyle had assisted on a case she and West had worked on. They both knew he didn't lend his skills on a regular basis. "I know he doesn't have a record, but are the feds keeping an eye on him? Or his Warrior Society?"

West dusted the salt from his fingers. "There's a file on the society and Kyle's name is in it."

She scooted to the edge of her chair. "Has he or anyone else been linked to any crimes?"

"Nothing that can be proven."

"But there's speculation?"

"Yes."

"What kind of speculation?" she asked.

West blew out a rough breath. "If you want to know what Kyle is up to, then you should ask him."

She merely blinked. Suddenly the special agent was snubbing her, refusing to share information. "You're protecting him from me? *You,* of all people."

"He helped when I was sick."

"I helped, too." Frustrated, she put down her drink. Although some people would find it hard to believe, West had been infected with an object-intrusion spell, a Native American witchcraft tool that had nearly killed him. But that was eight months ago, and he was well now. "When did you check to see if there was a file on him?" she asked. "Before or after he helped you?"

"After. But I was curious about him before."

"And now I'm curious."

"That's understandable." West finished his beer. "But I'm not going to betray him. Not with the woman he's sleeping with."

"How noble of you. How male. How Indian," she added, lacing her voice with sarcasm.

"Don't even go there, Riggs. I'm not that kind of Indian."

"Aren't you?" Although he wasn't an activist like Kyle, he was a mixed-blood registered with his tribe. And on top of that, Olivia probably influenced him. She'd done her fair share of fighting for Native causes.

"You know damn well I'm not," he countered.

Joyce didn't respond. West had never touted his heritage in front of her. By most people's standards, he didn't even look Indian. But sitting across from him now, he made her feel white.

"Ask Kyle," he pressed. "Talk to him about this."

She reached for her drink and plucked the cherry out of it, placing it on the cocktail napkin beside her. "Fine. But do you really think he is going to be honest with me?"

"If he cares about you, he will," West said, leaving her with a lump in the back of her throat.

"I was getting worried," Kyle told Joyce as he unlocked the gate that led to his property. "I expected you before now."

"We never specified a time." She glanced at his companions. Clyde stood patiently, and Bonnie danced around Joyce's feet. She knelt to pet the wiener dog, then looked up at Kyle.

He wore varying shades of denim and a battered fringe jacket reminiscent of the Vietnam War era. A slight breeze tousled his hair.

"I fixed lunch," he said.

Her heart made a foolish flutter. This wasn't the time to get girlish over him. Yesterday they'd agreed to spend some casual time together, but today she had an ulterior motive. "You cooked for me?"

"I made sandwiches. For a picnic," he added.

"Really?" She hadn't pegged him for the picnic type. "Where?"

"In the laser tag compound."

"That sounds fun." And it made her feel guilty, even if she knew she had the right to question him about his Warrior Society activities.

They walked to his house, and he retrieved their late-day lunch. From there, they took his Jeep to the airplane hangar that supported the laser tag course. The dogs came with them.

Once they went inside, Joyce marveled at the genius of the structure. The building was equipped with a variety of movie props and set changes, including lifelike audio tracks and devices that scented the air and altered the weather.

She glanced up. At the moment, the painted sky was sunny and the temperature was warm.

"I can make it rain," Kyle said.

"At a picnic?"

"We could huddle in a cave." He gestured to a stone path that led to a mountainlike formation.

Indoor rain sounded sexy, but she wasn't sure if it was a good idea. Sooner or later, she was going to ask him if he was involved in criminal activity, and a sunny day seemed safer somehow.

"I'd prefer a dry picnic," she said.

He removed his jacket. "Then come with me."

She walked beside him with the dogs in tow. They crossed a small bridge and stopped in an area that was designed to look like a meadow. Faux flowers colored the grasslike ground, creating an alluring effect.

Bonnie ran ahead of them, and Joyce laughed. Clyde was too macho to make mad dash for the fake foliage, but he watched his canine friend kick up her heels.

Joyce and Kyle sat in the middle of the floral field. An electronic bird winged above their heads, and she admired its realistic flight.

"That's part of the magic," he told her.

Strange magic, she thought. She knew he played war games here. "I'll bet it's booby-trapped."

"Could be." He spread his jacket on the ground and setup their picnic, removing items from a duffel bag.

He'd packed more than sandwiches. She noticed cheese and crackers, too. And containers filled with various fruits and salads. For their beverage, he'd brought bottled water.

Joyce tasted her sandwich, a hearty roll with roast beef, avocado, tomato and lettuce. "This is good."

"Just because I hate to clean my kitchen doesn't mean I can't fix a halfway decent meal." He scooped one of the salads onto a paper plate for her. "Try the pasta."

She took a bite, impressed by the raw vegetables and spicy Italian dressing he'd added to the curly noodles. "A man of many talents."

"That's me." He leaned forward to kiss her, planting a chaste peck on her lips.

She wanted to kiss him for real, but her guilt had kicked in again, so she pretended that she wasn't craving more. Or that she wasn't stalling, stopping herself from asking him about his Warrior Society.

When he sat back, Bonnie climbed onto his lap. He petted the tiny pooch, then set her on her feet. As for Kyle's feet, Joyce noticed that he was wearing his moccasins.

She gestured with her fork. "Did someone make those for you?"

"Someone? Like who?"

"A female relative," she suggested. "Or an old lover."

"I made them. I'm crafty that way. Domestic slob that I am."

He was more than crafty, she thought. He was a loner. A man who'd learned to cook and sew to prove that he didn't need a woman tending to his needs.

As for cleaning…

"You should hire a housekeeper," she told him.

"My grandmother thinks I should find a wife."

Joyce sucked in a breath. Like the troubled woman she was, her mind strayed in a husbandly direction. Why did it matter how Kyle lived his life? She'd known he was a suspicious character when she'd first met him.

"The grandmother with the robe like mine?" she asked.

"Yep, that's her." He flashed a silly smile. "Grandma Ugly Robe."

She looked at him, her emotions still acting up. Why did his lifestyle matter? Because she was sleeping with him. And because in her own stupid way, she was getting attached.

"My baby sister thinks I should invite you to our parents' anniversary party," she said, wanting to clear the air, to admit that she'd told someone in her family about him.

"Really? So are you going to invite me?"

"It depends on how honest you are."

"About what?"

"Criminal activity."

For a moment, he merely stared at her. "What the hell is that supposed to mean?"

"Don't play dumb, Kyle. The FBI has a file on your Warrior Society."

"Of course they do." A muscle twitched in his jaw, and his faithful rottweiler sat down beside him, aware of his agitation. "The feds don't trust guys like me."

"Then why should I trust you?"

He stared at her once again. "I never claimed you should."

She held his gaze. "Is that an admission of guilt?"

"No."

"The FBI has been speculating about your activities."

He wrapped up his half-eaten sandwich and shoved it into the duffel bag. "Who told you that?"

"Special Agent West. But before you start cursing him, he wouldn't tell me what those speculations are."

Kyle crossed his arms. "Why? What's his agenda?"

"I don't think he has one. Other than not wanting to betray you to the woman you're sleeping with." She glanced at the spray of rainbow flowers, wishing they were real, wishing they could give her comfort. "He also thinks that if you cared about me, you'd tell me the truth."

"That's not right." He looked around the fake meadow, too. Avoiding her gaze. Avoiding the discomfort between them. "West shouldn't have said that."

"No, I suppose he shouldn't have." But he did, and the words made her ache. As foolish as it was, she wanted Kyle to care about her.

* * *

Kyle couldn't sleep. He sat up in bed and glanced at the clock: 2:24. He picked up the phone, then set it down. He couldn't call Joyce at this hour. Could he?

He got up, went down the hall to the bathroom and splashed some water on his face. He looked like hell, like a man haunted by a woman.

When he returned to his room, the clock said 2:25.

Screw it. He climbed back into bed and grabbed the phone again. He was going to call her. With a frown, he punched out the numbers.

The ringing on the other end of the line made his stomach jolt. Finally she answered.

"Hello?" She sounded anxious, as if she were expecting an emergency. Or a homicide-oriented call, something related to her job.

Which wasn't that far off the mark. She would probably want to kill him for interrupting her sleep.

"It's me," he told her.

"Kyle? Do you know what time it is?"

He stole another glance at the clock: 2:27 and counting. "Yes."

"And?" she pressed, waiting for him to explain.

He envisioned her sitting up in bed, too. Only her bed was soft and scented, with pastel sheets and a virginal quilt. He wished he were there, nuzzling her naked body. "Can I come over?"

She blew out an annoyed breath. "No."

"Why not?"

"Because I'm not giving in every time you have a sexual whim."

"Why not?"

"*Kyle.*"

A slight laugh sounded in her voice, and he smiled. He liked making her laugh. He liked making love to her, too. But that wasn't why he'd called. "I am starting to care about you, Joyce."

Silence. Then, "You are?"

"Of course I am. I wouldn't be spending all this time with you if I wasn't." He kicked away the covers. "Are you starting to care about me?"

"Yes."

"Enough to let me come over?"

She turned suspicious. "What for?"

"To talk." His stomach jolted again, just a little, just enough to prove how she affected him. "Would it matter if I cared about you in the way West suggested?"

"Of course it would." Her voice perked up. "Are you offering to come clean? To discuss the Warrior Society?"

He made a face, hoping he wasn't going to regret this decision. That she wouldn't turn on him like the cop she was. "Yes, but you have to promise to come clean, too. To talk about your personal problems."

She stalled, sighing into the phone. "I never expected you to strike a bargain."

"Too bad. Take it or leave it."

Another sigh. "That's going to be difficult for me."

"And me opening up to a detective isn't?" Once he spilled his guts, she could hang him out to dry. Screw him over but good. "I'm not giving you something for nothing. Either we trust each other or we don't."

"This is scary," she said.

No kidding, he thought. "Are you game?"

When she cleared her throat and said, "Yes," he reached for his clothes and told her he would be over in about an hour. The drive would take him at least that long.

Kyle arrived at Joyce's apartment wearing a pair of jeans, an old sweatshirt and the moccasins he'd made. His hair was loose and getting in his eyes. He noticed the skeleton on the door was no longer blindfolded. The fabric was tied around its head instead.

Joyce opened the door before Kyle could knock or ring the bell.

"Hi," she said.

"Hi." He entered her living room. She was wearing her ugly robe and a nightgown beneath it. He'd assumed that she slept naked when she was alone, but apparently he was wrong. It didn't matter, he supposed. He liked the satiny nightgown, even if he couldn't see all of it.

They gazed at each other, and he hated how awkward this was.

"Where do you want to talk?" she asked.

"In bed. But we can keep our clothes on," he added, reminding her that this wasn't about sex.

She agreed, and he followed her to her room.

It looked as inviting as he remembered. The lights burned low, and the perfume bottles on her vanity table glinted with cut-glass allure, the shapes and see-through colors catching his eye. Her gun was there, too. Just like last time.

He turned to look at her, and she tucked her hair behind her ears. She seemed nervous, but he knew this was more intimate than sex. More revealing. They'd just agreed to confide in each other, to unearth their secrets.

Kyle waited for her to shed her robe and climb into bed. Once she did, he removed his moccasins and took the spot next to her.

By now, it was nearly four in the morning.

"I'm glad you don't have to work tomorrow," he said, wondering if the nature of her job ever chilled her in the middle of the night, if she saw murder victims in her sleep. "It's good that you have time off."

Her eyes locked onto his. "It's turning into a strange vacation."

"Because of me?"

She nodded. "You're deeper than I thought you were. More complex."

"So are you." He was itching to touch her, but he kept his hands to himself.

"You have to go first, Kyle."

"I know." He felt as though they were playing a soul-searching game of Truth or Dare, and they'd both picked Truth. "Maybe you should ask me some questions. Get the ball rolling that way."

"Fine." She took an audible breath. "Do you know what the FBI is speculating about you? About your Warrior Society?"

He turned to face her. "They probably think we steal."

She frowned at him. "And do you?"

"That depends on a person's perceptive." He watched her adjust the quilt. They were both leaning against the headboard. "We've been known to retrieve sacred objects and return them to their rightful owners."

"Why don't the rightful owners have legal possession of these objects? There are laws to protect them. Federal and state enactments."

"Yes, but it's not as simple as it sounds. I know of a tribe, here in California, who spent five years, back and forth with the federal government, trying to re-obtain something from a university that's sacred to their Nation. Something the university considered research material."

"So what are you saying? That in these types of situations the Warrior Society offers to help? To steal back what belongs to them?"

"Yes, but most Nations don't take us up on our offer. Not when a tribal council is involved."

"Because they're smart," she said. "They know better than to get involved in illegal activity."

He shrugged. "It doesn't matter. We've got enough missions to keep us busy. Mostly we focus on private collectors who claim that they don't have items that are supposed to be returned. Collectors who manage to elude the law altogether, who are keeping things that were robbed from graves."

"That's a noble cause, Kyle. But you can't just go around breaking into people's homes, looking for funerary objects."

"Why not? Someone stole them to begin with."

"Then do whatever you can to prove your case," she argued. "To expose these collectors and reobtain the objects legally." She paused, frowned a little. "Even if it takes years."

"We've tried that in the past, and the investigations have gone nowhere."

"So instead, you put yourself in the position of getting arrested for breaking and entering? Or getting shot and killed during a robbery attempt?"

"Yes," he responded honestly.

She sighed, and he could see that she didn't understand. That she didn't think the crime was worth the consequence.

He snared her gaze. "Do you think it's right that someone should disrespect a little girl's bones, that her skeleton should be hidden somewhere?"

"No. Of course not."

"We'll that's my current mission," he told her. "There's a private collector, an older man with tons of money, who we believe has the skeleton of an Indian child."

Joyce fussed with the quilt, and he could see that he'd unnerved her.

"I know the child's name," he said. "I know what century she was born in and when she died. And now I want to return her to her descendents, so she can be buried. So she can find peace."

"Then let me help you. We can discuss it with Agent West. We can—"

"No." He stopped her before she could continue. "I'm doing this my way. No paperwork. No red tape. No federal raids that turn up nothing."

She shook her head. "You don't have any faith in law enforcement."

He squinted at her. "Does that offend you?"

"It makes me worry. I don't want you to do something that will get you in trouble." She searched his gaze. "Will you promise me something?"

He didn't respond. Instead he waited for her to continue.

She did, only a second later. "Promise that you won't steal anything while we're still dating. No breaking and entering. No crimes."

Damn, he thought. Talk about getting screwed. "That's asking a lot, Detective."

"I can't condone what you do. I can't be with a man who's breaking the law."

"I just want to bring a little girl's remains home."

"I know. And I understand how you feel. But it's not the moral issue that concerns me. It's you getting busted. Or hurt. Or hurting someone else."

"I'd never participate in an armed robbery."

"You don't need a weapon," she countered. "You're an expert at unarmed combat."

"I would never hurt anyone. That's not what my missions are about."

She glared at him. "Either make the promise or say no."

Kyle knew this was his fault for admitting the truth, for telling a cop his secrets. But he was willing to accept responsibility, at least for while. "Fine. No crimes, not while I'm with you." He wasn't ready for their relationship to end. Not yet. "But later, when this thing between us is over, I'm doing whatever I want."

"Go ahead. But if you get busted, don't come cry-ing to me."

He relaxed a little. Apparently she wasn't going to turn him in, run to the feds with the information he'd given her. "Now you can tell me about your personal problems. You can come clean."

Suddenly her expression changed. She made a face, then fussed with the quilt again. "Can it wait?"

He gauged the anxiety in her gestures. She was on overload, he thought. They both were. "Until when?"

"Until we get some sleep." She glanced at the clock. "We've been up all night."

Like an idiot, he caved in. "I suppose a few more hours won't make a difference." He wanted to know what was going on in her life, but he wanted to hold her, too. To let the moment settle, to let their emo-tions slip into slumber.

She fluffed her pillow, getting ready to lie down. "Thank you, Kyle."

"For what?" He removed his sweatshirt, but de-cided to leave his jeans on.

"Everything," she responded.

He accepted her answer. In his heart, he knew how important his honesty had been to her.

Together, they adjusted the covers. And when she closed her eyes, he reached for her, and she snuggled against him. They were a strange couple, he thought. But for now, he liked being with her, even if they were as mismatched as two people could get.

Nine

Joyce woke up beside Kyle. She turned on her side to look at him. He was still asleep, with his hair partially covering his face and the sheet draped around his waist.

She wanted to run her hand along his chest and down his stomach, but this wasn't the time to get sexual. She'd promised to talk about her problems.

She sat up, her nerves jangling. It was foolish to be worried. Her secret wasn't as damaging as his. He'd admitted that he was involved in illegal activity. All she was going to do was admit that she was longing to get married and have a baby. That was a far cry from telling a detective that you steal.

Kyle never ceased to amaze her. He'd offered information about himself that very few people would entrust to a cop. Which meant what? That the bond between them was growing stronger? That he wanted her to know what he was willing to risk his freedom for?

A little girl's bones, she thought. A child's remains.

Joyce tried not to get attached to the dead, to the victims associated with her job. But sometimes she did. Sometimes her emotions got in the way. Apparently Kyle had become attached to "his" little girl, a child that had probably been born over a hundred years ago.

She gave in and touched him, placing her hand against his chest, against the warm, steady beats of his heart. Then she slipped lower, brushing the waistband of his jeans.

He opened his eyes, squinting at her, and she flinched. Guilty pleasure, she thought. She'd gotten caught with her hand in the cookie jar.

Well, not *in* the cookie jar. But darn close.

"What are you doing?" he asked.

"Nothing." She took her hand away.

His lips quirked. "It felt like something to me."

She changed the subject. "Do you want some coffee? I'm going to make a pot."

"Sure." He sat up and smoothed his hair. "Did you know that I left some condoms in your bathroom from last time?"

"You did? Where?"

"Under the sink, behind your tampons."

Good grief. "We don't need them right now."

He grinned. "The tampons?"

She couldn't find the will to laugh. "The condoms." She got out of bed, her nerves jumping like frogs in a pond. "You didn't come over to have sex, remember?"

"Yeah, I remember." His grin faded. "Are you okay, Joyce?"

"I'm fine." Just fretful about telling him her secret. In her own anxiety-ridden way, she wanted to make love with him before she spilled the beans, before she started talking about babies. But she knew that would be cheating. The true test of their affair would come after she told him. After he knew her biological clock was ticking.

Not that he was going to offer to give her a baby. No, she thought. He would never do that. If anything, he would panic and consider running for the door.

Of course she had no business imagining him as the father of her unborn children.

None whatsoever.

Joyce left to make the coffee, and he waited for her. When she returned with two steaming cups, she handed Kyle his, knowing he liked it black.

"Thanks." He scooted over so she could rejoin him in bed.

She took her designated spot and sipped the hot brew. The quiet laziness appealed to her. And so did having a big, rugged, rumpled male next to her.

"You're going to think I'm crazy," she said, getting ready to tell him her story.

He shrugged, then smiled. "All cops are crazy."

"Not like me." She blew out the breath she'd been holding, expanding her lungs. "I keep freaking out about wanting a baby."

His smile disappeared. Just like that. It was gone. "Is this a joke?"

"No."

"That's why you wanted to train with me? To stop yourself from hungering after a kid?"

She winced. Then abandoned her coffee. Her stomach had begun to burn. "And a husband. I want to get married, as well."

He winced, too. But kept his coffee. "You are crazy."

"I told you."

"We sparred over your domestic urges?" He gulped the caffeine-laced beverage, swallowing a bit too loudly. "That makes me feel weird."

She could see the panic setting in. He even glanced at the door, as if he wanted to bolt. "I'm pushing forty, Kyle. These things happen to women."

"These things?"

"Biological-clock issues. Besides, remember what

you said the other morning? That given my family history, you expected me to be more marriage-minded?"

"Maybe so. But I didn't think that was the trauma in your life." His eyebrows furrowed, working into a frown. "I made a promise to you last night, and now you have to make one to me."

She angled her head. "What?"

"That you don't start caring about me too much."

Pride kicked her square in the gut, a swift blow, a wallop she couldn't deny. And on top of that, a strap on her nightgown had begun to slip. She pushed it back into place, wishing she wasn't wearing such a girly garment. "What's that supposed to mean? That you think I'm dumb enough to fall in love with you?"

"I'm not that bad. That unlovable." He seemed irritated, too. "I have my moments."

"You could have fooled me."

"Yeah, listen to you. You're hot for me."

She narrowed her eyes. "No hotter than you are for me."

"Okay. Whatever." He accepted their attraction on equal ground. "How about if we both agree not to fall in love? Not to make more of this than it is?"

She wasn't about to argue. She didn't want to fall for Kyle any more than he wanted to fall for her. "That's fine with me."

"Do you want to shake on it?" he asked.

She gave him a stupefied look. "This isn't a business arrangement."

"You're right. There's no point in going overboard." He set his cup on the nightstand. "Shaking hands would be kind of goofy. Maybe we could mess around to seal the deal."

Suddenly she forgot about being annoyed with him. She laughed instead, enjoying his offbeat charm. "Is that all you think about?"

He laughed, too. "It seems like it, huh? It must be your effect on me."

And his effect on her, she thought. She feared that getting him out of her system wouldn't be as easy as it sounded.

He flopped onto his pillow and took her hand. She put her head on her pillow, too. And for a while, they didn't speak.

Nothing. No words. No jokes. No sexual innuendos. Just a closeness they weren't supposed to share.

Finally he turned to face her. He was still holding her hand. "You're going to find the right guy someday."

Something inside her ached. Horribly. "You think so?"

"Yeah, I do. You'll be married with a baby before you turn forty."

"I don't know. At this point, I'd rather fight off those feelings."

"And tie yourself up in knots. That's not worth it, Joyce. Just let it happen when it's meant to."

It was good advice, she thought. Sound. Kind. Everything she needed to hear. He was a levelheaded man. Or he could be, when the mood struck him. "I can't imagine why Olivia's sister thinks you're dumb."

"What?" The change of topic threw him.

"Olivia's sister, Allie. She thinks you're dumb."

"No, she doesn't. Not anymore. I've been training her for nearly a year. She knows now how brilliant I am." He chuckled. "She's the airhead. Addle-brain Allie."

Joyce took her hand away and pinched him. "You're not supposed to call her that."

"Even if it's true?"

She rolled her eyes. The first disagreement they'd ever had was about his nickname for Allie. And that was on the day they'd met. Eight months ago, she thought. And now here she was, in bed with him.

Better her than Olivia. Or Allie. Or any other woman he was associated with.

She moved closer, snuggling against him, against the warmth of his flesh, the roughness of his jeans. "I think we're going to need those condoms you left in the bathroom."

He guided her hand to his pocket. "I already snagged one when you were in the kitchen. Just in case."

"What a cheater." She dug into the denim, bumping his fly in the process. "A sexy cheater." She secured the packet and glanced at the ridge beneath his zipper. "Did I do that?"

"You know damn well you did." He toyed with her nightgown, fingering the silky trim. Then he removed it, slowly, sensually, baring her breasts and exposing her panties.

When the air hit her skin, her nipples turned hard. He kissed her, then cupped her breasts, making them ache. She closed her eyes and let him put his hands all over her.

He was gentler than she expected, gentler than any man who'd ever touched her. She wanted to tell him to stop being so loving, so caring, but she didn't think he realized what he was doing.

She opened her eyes, and he discarded her panties. They were pink, like cotton candy, and she could have sworn they'd melted into thin air.

He undressed himself and pressed his nakedness against hers. The sensation made her shiver. All she wanted to do was hold him, keep him close.

They rolled over the bed, the covers bunching beneath them. Colors swirled in her mind, as pale and pastel as the sheets.

"Will you give me a key to your apartment?" he asked.

She blinked. "Why?"

"For when you go back to work. So I can come

over when you're not home and wait for you." He straddled her, nudging her thighs apart. "I'll give it back when we're not together anymore."

She agreed to give him a key. At this point, she would deny him nothing.

He used the protection, and they made warm, syrupy love. She gripped his shoulders and felt the moisture between her legs, the stimulation of each and every stroke. He penetrated her even deeper, and she lost her breath.

He filled her so fully, so completely, the lines between them blurred.

And when they climaxed at the same moment, at the very same instant, the rest of the world seemed to disappear, fading into nothingness.

Like the edges of a dream.

Kyle and Joyce spent the rest of the afternoon together. They took a shower, soaping each other down, then got dressed and headed to Santa Monica. Kyle loved the sand and the surf. The weather was overcast, bordering on drizzly, but that made it even better. To him, the beach was prettier in the fall and winter months of the year.

They stood on the pier and looked out at Pacific Park, with its oceanview Ferris wheel and other family-entertainment rides. The park was closed, but this was a weekday during an off-season.

He glanced down. The boardwalk itself was separated into two distinct sections. Part of it was made of wood, and the other part offered a long, asphalt surface, where a few locals were fishing. Overall, there weren't a lot of people around.

As Kyle and Joyce walked past the police pier substation, he slanted her an amused look. "I can't seem to get away from cops."

"No, you can't, can't you?" She took his hand, and they continued their stroll.

Suddenly he realized the magnitude of their relationship. He'd agreed to halt his upcoming mission—albeit temporarily—for her.

He frowned, and she turned to look at him. "What's wrong?" she asked.

"Nothing." He stopped to watch the wind blow her hair around her face. She looked pretty in the cloudy light. "Nothing I can't deal with later." He paused, inhaling the moisture in the air. "Do you want go down to the beach? Maybe walk on the sand?"

She nodded. "Sure."

They took a set of cement stairs and reached the bottom, where Mother Earth presented a close-up view of the Pacific Ocean. The sand felt right beneath Kyle's moccasins. He wore the same clothes he'd worn to Joyce's apartment last night. She was dressed in a similar way, with jeans and a sweatshirt. Her shoes were lace-up boots.

"I used to come here when I was a teenager," he said. "When I got stuck living with my dad. But I always came here on cold days or at night. I didn't like it as much when it was sunny and crowded."

"What about now?"

"I still prefer it when there's less people around."

"I like the beach either way," she said. "Summer days can be fun, too. The street performers, the hot dogs, the lemonade, music blaring from boom boxes."

He led her along an endless stretch of land, close to the shore, but far enough away not to get their feet wet. "I'd probably come here in the summer if I had a family. It'd be fun to haul my kids to the beach. To teach them to build sand castles or something."

She stopped walking. "I thought you didn't want to get married and have children."

"I don't." He noticed how blue her eyes were, how they reflected the ocean. "I was just saying it hypothetically."

She seemed to be focused on his eyes, too. "I wish you wanted kids."

He tried not to react, but his pulse made a disconcerting leap. "Why?"

"So you would understand how I feel."

"I do understand. I said you were going to find the right guy someday. Someday in the near future," he added.

"Before I'm forty." She laughed a little. "Everyone seems to worry about the big four-oh. Especially single women." She considered him. "How do you know that I'm going to find the right guy? You're not psychic."

"No, but I have common sense. You're beautiful and tough and sexy. A lot of men would want to settle down with a lady like you."

She shrugged and turned away to look at the ocean. He wasn't sure if she believed him.

"Maybe I should ask Olivia," he said.

She spun back around. "Ask her what?"

"When you're going to find the guy of your dreams."

"Don't you dare," she warned. "Don't you dare ask her."

"Why not? She's a damn good psychic. If anyone would know—"

"Don't do it, Kyle. Don't involve her in my petty problems."

"They're not petty, Joyce. This baby-thing is tearing you apart."

"I'm learning to cope." She grazed the side of his face, skimming her fingers along his jaw. "And you're helping me. My diversion. My sparring partner. My roll-in-the-hay lover."

He smiled at her. Her touch felt good, soft and sweet. "We haven't done it in a hay loft."

"So we'll find a barn somewhere."

"Yeah, right." He couldn't help but scoff. "As if you'd be willing to do it someplace where we could get caught."

"Okay, so maybe we'll have to skip the hay." She leaned in to kiss him, to make the moment warm and sensual.

He put his arms around her, and they held each other, with the wind blowing and the sea crashing in foamy waves. She nuzzled his neck, and he breathed in her perfume, a floral fragrance from her vanity table. He couldn't remember the name of it, but he'd watched her spray it on earlier that day.

When they separated, he was strangely aroused. More emotionally than sexually, something he didn't quite understand.

"Are you going to invite me to your parents' anniversary party?" he asked.

She gave him a surprised look. "I wasn't sure if you'd want to go."

"I'm curious to meet your family. But if you're uncomfortable taking me—"

"No. I'd like you to be there. Besides, if I don't bring you, I'll get roped into a blind date. My youngest sister threatened to set me up with her husband's boss."

A snap of masculine rivalry lashed across his chest, across his annoyed heart. He didn't want her dating anyone else, not while she was sleeping with him. "Some corporate dude, I'll bet."

"The suit-and-tie type." She bumped his arm. "Jealous?"

"No."

She seemed disappointed. "Not even a little?"

"I don't know. Maybe." He bumped her right back. "You're supposed to be mine for a while. At least until Halloween."

"Why Halloween?"

"So we can hand out candy together. At your apartment. No one trick or treats at my house."

"With the locked fence and the big, black guard dog? Gee, I can't imagine why."

"Smart aleck." He dug his moccasins into the sand. "When is the anniversary party?"

"It's on the Saturday before Halloween."

"Then it's perfect timing. I can come in costume. I can be an Indian. A big, bad Apache."

"Very funny." She grabbed his waist and pulled him tight against her, initiating a kiss.

For now, he thought, they owned the beach: the sea, the grainy soil, the shells scattered upon the shore. This was their moment, their forbidden romance, their affair.

She tasted like heaven, like everything he wanted, everything he needed. But it wasn't meant to last.

They'd both agreed not to fall in love.

Ten

Two weeks later, Kyle got ready for the anniversary shindig. He'd agreed to meet Joyce at the party because she'd gone early to help with the food and whatnot.

And now he was stressed out about arriving alone, about being judged by her family, about why he'd persuaded her to invite him in the first place.

His affection for her was getting the best of him.

After her vacation had ended and she returned to her job, he started missing her. She worked long, grueling hours. They barely got to spend any time together, just a few stolen hours, a few late-night lovemaking sessions.

And at the moment, it didn't seem like enough.

He glanced at Clyde. The rottweiler was sitting on the bedroom floor, watching him. Bonnie was there, too.

"I should know better," he said out loud.

The dogs, of course, didn't answer. They merely let him talk, let him vent in front of the mirror, where he tucked his shirt into his pants.

"She's all I think about. Me, hooked on a cop." He turned to address his companions. "How stupid is that?"

Clyde didn't react, but Bonnie perked her ears.

Kyle blew out an anxious breath, then finished getting dressed. He'd already pulled his hair into a ponytail because he thought it made him look more respectable, more reserved, if that were possible.

He went outside to get in his Jeep, and the dogs followed him to the yard, where they stayed to protect the property. Bonnie seemed to think her teeny-weeny presence made a difference. Kyle didn't have the heart to tell her otherwise.

He drove to the San Fernando Valley, where Joyce's parents lived. Their house was a two-story structure with a manicured lawn, several shady trees and a brick flowerbed.

As he neared the front door, he could hear jovial sounds of the party in progress. Luckily it wasn't a formal affair. But it wasn't a barbecue, either. It was somewhere in between, or at least that was what Joyce had told him.

He knocked, and a young woman answered. She was blonde, cute and curious. He noticed her checking him out.

"You must be Kyle," she said.

And she must be the baby of the family, he thought. The one who had threatened to set Joyce up with the corporate dude.

He nodded, affirming who he was. "It's obvious, I guess."

"Completely." She extended a greeting. "I'm Jessica, Joyce's sister. There are six of us altogether. All 'J' names." She paused to look him over again. "You're not Joyce's usual type."

"I know. She prefers a suit and tie." He met her gaze. "Or she used to. I think she prefers me now."

"You're right. She does. She would never admit it, but she's been chomping at the bit for you to show up."

Good, he thought. "Is your husband's boss here?" he asked, letting Jessica know that he'd heard about the other man.

"No." She sent him an impish grin. "But I'm glad it matters to you."

He didn't deny her claim. For now, it did matter. The lady cop was his lover, and he wasn't ready to give her up. He should be, but he wasn't.

Jessica linked her arm through his. "Come on. I'll take you to Joyce and she can introduce you around."

She led him inside, and he caught sight of a spacious living room, a colorful kitchen and a glass sunroom. The other guests were everywhere, socializing with drinks and appetizers.

He didn't have to glance around to know that quite a few people had taken notice of him. He was big and tall. He always made an impression.

Suddenly he saw Joyce. There she was, surrounded by family and friends, talking and smiling. She sat in a wicker chair in the sunroom, bouncing a baby on her lap. He couldn't tell how old the child was, but a pink headband bow and frilly dress gave away her gender.

Joyce glanced up and noticed him from across the room. As they stared at each other, the afternoon sun streaked between them, making the glass enclosure seem even brighter.

"Dang," Jessica said. "You two are intense."

Embarrassed, Kyle broke the trance. He'd forgotten the younger woman was still standing beside him.

Joyce left her chair and came toward him, taking the baby girl with her.

"I'm glad you finally made it," she said, when they were only inches apart.

"I didn't mean to be late." He glanced at the child, and she gave him a slurpy smile. He couldn't help but smile back at her.

"That's my daughter," Jessica told him. "Her name is Gail."

"How old is she?" he asked.

"Seven months. Do you want to hold her?" Before he could respond, Joyce's sister reached for the baby and plunked her in his arms. "She loves everybody."

No kidding, he thought. Gail latched onto him, like a monkey to a tree, reaching around to grab his ponytail.

"Be good," her mamma said. "Don't pull his hair."

Gail didn't listen. She tugged on it, like she was yanking his chain. Then she put her head on his shoulder and cozied up to him.

Joyce watched him with the baby, a tender look in her eyes. "She's got your number."

He tried not to make too much of it. He'd already told Joyce that he appreciated kids. "She's just like her aunt." He smoothed Gail's ruffled dress. "Feisty one minute and sweet the next."

The lady cop smiled, and they stared at each other again. He knew half the people in the room were watching them, wondering who Joyce's new lover was, but he didn't care. For now, they were still a couple.

Soon the little girl in his arms nodded off, using him as a pillow. Jessica took her daughter, leaving him and Joyce alone.

"Are you ready to meet my parents?" she asked.

He wanted to say no, but he couldn't avoid the guests of honor. This party was for them. "Sure. Why not?"

She introduced him to her mom first, who was hanging out in the kitchen with a group of older women, where a buffet-style meal was being prepared.

"Mom, this is Kyle Prescott. Kyle, this is Alice Riggs, the saint who raised six girls and put up with my dad for forty years."

"Then I'm honored," he said, grateful for Joyce's wit.

Alice, a slightly plump blonde in her sixties, laughed and shook his hand, welcoming him with genuine warmth.

When he moved closer to Joyce, the older woman seemed pleased by his affection for her daughter. He felt a bit guilty, knowing he and Joyce had agreed not to fall in love. He didn't think Alice would understand a sex-only affair.

He met some of the other ladies in the kitchen and they were warm and friendly, too. But coming face-to-face with Joyce's father wasn't so easy.

They found him in the garage, where he and his cronies gathered around a vintage car.

Joyce made the introduction, but she didn't crack a joke, not this time. "Kyle, this is my father, Brock Riggs. Dad, this is Kyle Prescott."

The men shook hands. Brock stood about six feet, with good-size shoulders and short gray hair. He had steely blue eyes and a moustache, one that reminded Kyle of a parody of a seventies cop. All he needed was a pair of mirrored shades to go with it.

Joyce's dad was stuck in a time warp.

Amused, Kyle shifted his stance. He wanted to smile, but he didn't dare. Brock was giving him a critical study.

"My daughter told me you're a Desert Storm veteran."

Joyce had mentioned him? No doubt trying to soften the blow. "Yes, sir."

"She said you're highly decorated."

"I believe in serving my country."

Brock merely nodded. "I respect that."

"Thank you." He wanted to breathe a sigh of relief.

Or salute. Or get the hell out of here and never come back.

But then Brock offered him a beer, and he figured he'd passed the test. A second later, as Joyce's dad walked over to the ice chest, she slanted Kyle a grin that made him feel like they were in high school. He gave in and grinned, too.

Brock turned around and caught them.

The older man's moustache twitched, but that was as close as his lips came to forming a smile. But for Kyle, it was enough. More than he'd expected from a retired cop who seemed hell-bent on protecting his only unmarried daughter.

* * *

After the party, Joyce dropped off her car at her apartment, changed into comfy clothes and packed a small bag. Kyle had invited her to spend the night with him, and she couldn't resist. Especially since he claimed that he had a surprise for her.

She sat next to him in his Jeep, analyzing the way he'd interacted with her family. Her parents accepted him, and her sisters and their husbands seemed to like him, too. But most of all, her nieces and nephews adored him. He'd played video games with the older kids, while the little ones had approached him with awe, bringing him their toys.

No wonder Joyce had slipped back into the marriage/baby mode. She had it bad. And it was Kyle's fault.

Of course he hadn't done it purposely. She couldn't hold her emotions against him.

He slanted her a quick glance. "I had a good time. Better than I thought I would."

"I'm glad you were there." And sad that sooner or later, he would disappear from her life. "So what's my surprise?"

He changed lanes, getting ready to exit the freeway. "If I told you, it wouldn't be a surprise. Besides, it's not that big of a deal. Just one of my whims."

"I'll bet you cleaned your house."

"Then you're going to be disappointed." He took the off-ramp that led to a desert highway. "It's still a mess."

She sat back in her seat, unable to figure out what he was up to. She supposed that was one of things she enjoyed about him. No one could call him predictable.

When they arrived at his house, he unlocked the vehicle-entry gate and drove straight to the airplane hangar.

"My surprise is in there?" she asked.

He smiled. "You're awfully curious, Detective."

"That's precisely why I'm a detective." She unbuckled her seat belt. "My inquisitive nature."

They entered the laser tag course, which at the moment, was pitch black. Joyce nearly bumped into Kyle, and he chuckled.

He flipped on the lights, but nothing spectacular happened. From her vantage point, everything looked the same as it had on the day of the picnic. Then again, in a building this big, she couldn't be sure.

"Let's go for a walk," he said. "We'll take this path."

She looked around, wondering if he'd turned the hangar into a haunted house. "Is it going to start raining? Or snowing?" She moved cautiously. "Or are the lights going to go out? Is something spooky going to jump out and grab me?"

He shook his head. "Ye of little faith. I would

never try to scare a woman who looks at pictures of dead people all day."

"I do more than that."

"Oh, that's right. You go to autopsies, too."

"That's not funny." Even if she had puked her guts up the first time she'd smelled a rotting corpse. "I help put killers behind bars."

"I know." He stopped walking. "And you work endless hours to do it."

She met his gaze. By now, they were near the faux-flower meadow. "I have tomorrow off."

"Which is why I intend to hold onto you tonight. To keep you for as long as I can."

"Oh." She softened her voice, touched by the tender possessiveness in his. "I guess that means you've been missing me."

"You have no idea." He took her hand and guided her around a fake wall.

And that was when she saw the hayloft. Instantly she knew it was her surprise.

"My roll-in-the-hay lover." She turned to smile at him. "You put that up for me."

"It gave me something to do while you were working all that overtime." He gestured to the enclosure. "Want to try it out?"

"Absolutely." She started up the stairs first. The entire structure was made of spruce logs, giving it a rustic quality. "Did you build this yourself?"

"Yes." He climbed the steps behind her. "I usually buy or lease the props in here, but I wanted to make this one."

To her, it was more than a prop. It was a heartfelt gift, something she would never forget.

Once they reached the top, they both dived into the scratchy bedding. Although it was warm and absorbent, it grazed their skin, clinging to their hair and clothes.

They looked at each other and laughed.

"This isn't what horses eat," he said. "This is what they sleep on."

"I know." She lifted a handful of the golden stalks, letting it flutter like rain. "I'm not that much of a city girl. I know the difference between hay and straw." She paused to contemplate her situation. "I guess this makes you my roll-in-the-straw lover."

Her leaned over her. "I guess it does."

She lay beneath him, studying the handsome angles of his face. "Did you really miss me that much?"

He nodded. "It frustrates me. Thinking about a woman when she isn't around."

"You don't seem frustrated now."

"Because you're here." He closed his hand over her blouse. "And I can touch you."

"You're good at that."

One by one, he released her buttons. He seemed so intense, so completely absorbed in what he was doing. He removed her tennis shoes and tugged on her jeans, determined to undress her.

When she was naked, he kissed her. A kiss so warm, so compelling, she wondered how she was ever going to replace him.

She undressed him, too. She wanted to explore his body, to roam his muscles, to skim his scars, the healed-over bullet wounds that marred his skin. She'd noticed them before, but she hadn't focused on them until now.

But tonight, everything seemed different.

More powerful. More real.

She circled the scar on his chest. "Is this from the war?"

He nodded.

"And this one?" She gestured to his leg. She knew Olivia had accidentally shot him.

"That was nothing, just a scratch." He studied her expression, her sneaky smile. "But apparently you already know that."

"Sorry, I couldn't help it." She removed a piece of straw from his hair. "Olivia told me about it."

"We've told each other things, too."

"You and her?"

He shook his head. "You and me. I've never confided in anyone like I have with you."

"Me, neither." Her pulse tripped and stumbled. Here she was in a makeshift hayloft with a man who'd become more than her playmate. He'd also become her dearest, most treasured friend.

"Are you ready for me?" he asked, holding her close, his body warm against hers.

"Yes." She knew he was talking about sex, about a physical joining. But for her, it was more than that.

Suddenly Joyce knew exactly what was happening. She was losing her heart.

To a man she'd vowed not to love.

Eleven

On Wednesday afternoon Kyle conducted a training session with Allie Whirlwind, Olivia's younger sister. He and Allie stood on a sparring mat in his gym, with barely any communication between them.

Kyle couldn't concentrate on the lesson.

"You're not paying attention," Allie said.

"Yes, I am," he lied.

"No, you're not." Peeved, she put her hands on her hips.

Kyle analyzed Allie. She was tall and lean with waist-length hair and striking features. He used to think she was hot, but over time she'd become like a little sister to him. He'd quit noticing her in a male-female sense. Not that she'd ever noticed him that way. Allie used to think he was dumb.

He squinted at her. Maybe he was dumb, at least dumb enough to keep lusting after a cop. Joyce was working today, putting in long hours, as usual.

And he couldn't quit thinking about her.

"What's wrong with you?" Allie asked.

"Nothing." He walked over to the mini fridge and removed two bottled waters, handing her one.

She frowned at the offering. "I'm not thirsty."

"Too bad. We're taking a break. Besides, you need to drink water during a session. I've told you that before. Getting dehydrated is a health risk."

She uncapped the bottle and took a small sip. "Maybe we should spar outside today. You're always going on and on about environmental training. New challenges. A change of scenery and all that."

"I don't want to go outside."

"Fine." She plopped down on the mat, sitting cross-legged, scowling at him.

Kyle wondered if he should end the session early, if he was wasting her time.

Suddenly she quit sulking. In an instant, her mood turned chipper. "I just figured out what's bugging you."

Great. Now he had to listen to one of her addle-brained theories. He adored Allie, but her constant chatter got on his nerves.

Her dark eyes lit up. "You're falling in love with Detective Riggs."

Kyle's breath rushed out. No way was he going to let Allie mess with his emotions, not about Joyce. Not about the pact they'd made. "You're full of crap."

"Yeah, right. It's written all over your face, lover boy."

"Keep it up and I'm going to knock you on your butt."

She lifted her hind-end a smidgen, raising one cheek in the air. "I'm already on my butt. And you're just getting ticked off because you know it's true."

He crossed his arms. "I made a promise to Joyce, and she made one to me. We agreed not to let it happen."

"That's ridiculous." She shook her head. "I'll bet Joyce has already figured out how she feels."

"No way."

"Yes, way. She's a detective. It's her nature to solve crimes." She grinned a little. "And her being in love with you is a crime. You're a terrible catch."

"I am not. I—" He stopped. He wasn't about to let her trick him into some sort of half-cocked admission. He was sexually obsessed with Joyce. She'd gotten under his skin. But that wasn't the same as being in love. "You're wrong, and I'm going to prove it." He grabbed her hand and dragged her up. "We're going to your house to talk to your sister. Olivia will set this straight."

"Why? Because she's psychic? I knew she was in love with West before she did. And I knew he loved her, too."

"It's different with Joyce and me." He nudged Allie toward the basement door, practically pushing her up the stairs. "There's another man in Joyce's future."

An hour later, Kyle and Allie sat across from Olivia in the loft where both women lived. To him, the mystic décor only intensified the moment: the velvet sofa, the fantasy mural, the scented candles.

"I don't like to delve into people's lives without their permission," Olivia said, denying his request.

"That's bull," Kyle retorted. "You do readings for police work all the time."

"Joyce isn't under investigation," she informed him.

"No, but your pain-in-the-carcass sister is claiming that Joyce and I are in love, and Joyce would hate that worse than an unauthorized reading."

Olivia sighed. "Why don't I do one on you instead?"

"Fine." He glanced at Allie, irked by the smug look on her face. "I've got nothing to hide."

Olivia left her chair and scooted between him and Allie on the couch. She took Kyle's hand and held it. He didn't say anything. He knew it was easier for her to get an accurate reading if she was touching someone. Of course, she could draw information from photographs, too. Or simply from her mind. Olivia was clairvoyant, clairaudient and empathic. In addition to having visions, she heard voices and sounds in her head. But her strongest gift was feeling other people's emotions.

She tilted her head, her expression difficult to discern. Her short, choppy hair fell in multiple layers, spiking around her face. Her psychic energy came from her ancestors. All of the women in her family, aside from her and Allie, were witches—a disgrace in their culture. But she and Allie had managed to overcome it.

Finally Olivia released his hand.

"Well?" he said.

She kept her expression blank. "You're the man Joyce is meant to be with."

He cursed, using the crudest word he could think of. "You're just saying that to side with Allie."

"No. I'm not. You're going to have a baby with her. A little girl."

"She's pregnant?" His stomach tensed, fear clawing at his gut. "But we used protection. We were careful. We—"

Olivia interrupted. "This baby hasn't been conceived yet. It isn't happening now. But it's part of your future." Her voice turned soft. "And Joyce is going to be an incredible mother."

He stood up, fighting the air in his lungs, struggling to breathe. He hadn't told Olivia about Joyce's secret. He hadn't told anyone.

"Is he going to be a good dad?" Allie asked her sister, while Kyle's knees nearly gave out.

"I don't know," the psychic answered. "My feelings didn't go in that direction."

"Hmm." Allie considered the situation. "I'll bet he will be. He's weird, but he—"

"Stop talking about me as if I'm not here." He rounded on both women, not surprised that their ancestors were witches. "You cooked up this little scheme, didn't you? You put your evil heads together and came up with a plan to coerce me into marrying Joyce."

Olivia rose to her feet, looking him in the eye. "Don't be such an imbecile. I have better things to do with my time."

"I told you he's always been a bit dense," Allie interjected. "But deep down he knows better. He's just scared, the way you were when you fell in love with West."

"I can't handle this." He couldn't picture himself as a husband and father. But worse yet, he couldn't imagine being married to an officer of the law, to a woman who would force him to conform, to change who and what he was. "I have to go."

"Where?" Allie called out after him. By now, he was halfway to the door.

To end his relationship with Joyce, he thought. To talk to her as soon as she got home. To stop Olivia's prediction from coming true.

After an exhausting day, Joyce walked into her apartment to find Kyle waiting for her. Surprised to see him, she set her belongings on a nearby end table. This was the first time he'd used the key she'd given him.

He rose from the couch and turned to look at her. Joyce's pulse zigzagged. Just knowing that she loved him made her nervous. Sweetly, strangely excited.

He blew out a rough breath, and she realized that he seemed anxious, too. But not in a good way. And in addition to that, he was wearing the kind of T-shirt and sweatpants he normally sparred in, which seemed odd.

"Did you come here to fight?" she asked.

He shook his head. "To talk. I've been here for hours."

Which meant he had something important on his mind. And instinct told her what it was. She didn't have to be a genius to figure it out, to read the expression on his face. "You don't want to be with me anymore, do you?"

He closed his eyes, squeezing them shut. Then he opened them. "Can we go outside? Maybe go for a walk so I can explain why?"

"Yes, of course." She prayed that she could keep

her emotions intact, that her eyes didn't water, that her voice didn't crack.

They left the apartment and headed down the stairs. From there, they took a cement path that cut across a greenbelt.

Dusk had fallen, leaving the October sky with a deep lavender hue. Joyce was dressed in black slacks and a matching blazer, and although the weather was mild, she fought a chill.

She glanced at Kyle and noticed his frown. She didn't have the courage to admit that she loved him. Not now. Not like this.

"I had a panic attack today," he said.

She stopped walking. "You did. Why?"

"Because of something Olivia said." He pulled a hand through his unbound hair. It flowed to his shoulders, rain-straight and as dark as the night. "I went to see her because I was trying to prove Allie wrong. Allie thinks the pact you and I made is stupid and that we're already in love."

Joyce struggled to respond. Suddenly everything inside her ached. "Allie has always been a dreamer."

"I know. And that's why I wanted Olivia to set her straight."

She buttoned her jacket, warding off another chill. "So what did Olivia say?"

"She did a reading on me. And—" He stalled, fidgeting with his hands, as if he didn't know what to do with them. His sweats didn't have pockets. "She messed with my mind. She told me that I was going to be the father of your baby. That we were going to have a little girl."

Joyce nearly swayed on her feet. "There's no way I'm pregnant. My menstrual cycle was on time."

"This little girl is supposed to be part of our future, a baby that hasn't been conceived yet." He stepped back. "Can you imagine us getting married? Raising a kid? You, a cop. Me, a guy who carries an illegal firearm and plots robberies. It would be insane."

She knew he was right, that as a couple they made no sense. But that didn't stop her from loving him, from wishing that he loved her, too.

"What if Olivia wasn't pulling a scam?" he said. "What if her prediction was real? What if you and I keep sleeping together and we make a baby?" He kept his distance, not standing too close. "I wouldn't know how to provide for a family, to be that stable. You should be with someone else."

Joyce didn't want anyone else. She wanted him. But she'd seen enough destruction to know that life didn't always give you want you wanted.

Still, she battled the hurt, the loneliness, the pain-wrenching loss. In her mind's eye, she could see the wedding they would never have, the mixed-blood daughter they would never conceive.

"I didn't even tell Olivia that you wanted kids." He

dropped his arms to his sides, and suddenly he seemed sad. "But she said you'd make an incredible mom. She didn't know if I'd make a good dad. That wasn't part of the reading."

She resisted the urge to cradle her womb, to clutch her middle. "Of course you would."

"Allie thinks so, too. Me and all my goofy toys, I guess." He took a step toward her, just one small, cautious step. "Do you understand why we shouldn't keep seeing each other, Joyce?"

She nodded, and her eyes filled with the tears she wasn't supposed to cry. Unsure of what else to do, she blinked, trying to will them away, trying to look strong and steady.

He reached out to touch her, but dropped his hand instead. "I'm sorry."

"Me, too." Her voice turned fragile, and she cursed her vulnerability. She longed to put her head on his shoulder, to grieve in his arms. But she wouldn't dare. She couldn't bear to fall apart in front of him. "You should go now. There's no point in hanging around."

"Promise me that you'll take care of yourself." He released an audible breath. "That you'll be happy. That you'll find the right guy."

"I will." She swallowed the lump in her throat, knowing she was lying. "Promise me that you won't get arrested. That you won't destroy your future."

He didn't respond. He just stood there.

And as the wind stirred, blowing a soft breeze around her face, she prayed that he would change his mind. That he would tell her that he'd fallen in love with her, that she was worth the risk, that he would alter his choices so he could marry a cop.

But he didn't.

He said goodbye and walked away, leaving her alone in the dark. She watched him until he disappeared, until there was nothing left but the emptiness in her heart.

Two days had passed and Kyle couldn't sleep. So he burned the late-night oil, rummaging through his storage sheds, looking for the Tiffany lamp he'd considered giving to Joyce.

He had no idea what he was going to do once he found the damn thing. Send it to her, he supposed. Along with the key to her apartment that he'd forgotten to return.

He cursed the dust that gathered on boxes, much in the way he'd been cursing himself. His mind had been straying in a dangerous direction. He could almost imagine planting a baby in Joyce's womb, giving her the child she wanted so desperately.

Which meant what? That he could imagine marrying her, too?

Yeah, right. As if he deserved to spend the rest of

his life with her. The sweet, beautiful detective he'd shackled and blindfolded. He sounded like a sado-masochist, not a loving, caring husband.

Finally he came across the carton he was searching for. Frustrated, he opened it with a pocketknife and removed the carefully packed object.

Mired in confusion, he stared at the stained-glass motif on the shade. Break a woman's heart, then send her an expensive antique? That made no sense.

He could tell how much he'd hurt Joyce. He'd seen the tears in her eyes. He'd heard the pain in her voice.

Was Allie right? Did Joyce love him? And what about himself? Was he too stubborn to admit that he was in love, too? Or too scared, as Allie had suggested?

He closed his eyes, wondering what he should do. Call Joyce? Go see her? Ask her to forgive him?

He didn't like being enthralled by a woman. It went against his nature, his big, bad macho lifestyle. But worse yet was not being with her at all.

His cell phone rang, jarring him from his thoughts. He checked the readout, hoping it was Joyce. But it wasn't. The display indicated that the caller was Allie.

He answered the summons, and her voice rushed over the line.

"Kyle? I tried your house, but you weren't there."

"I'm in one of my sheds." And it was late for her to be calling him. Almost midnight. "What's going on?"

"Have you seen Joyce? Is she with you?"

"No." Instantly alarmed, his pulse jumped to his throat. "Why? What's wrong?"

"I've been trying to reach her, but she's not answering her phone. Not her home number or her cell." Allie stalled for a second, then said, "I heard on the news that two police officers were shot this evening. I think one of them was a woman. Maybe even a detective."

Oh, God. He took a deep breath, warning himself not to panic. "Are you sure? Are you sure you heard the report correctly?"

"Not really, no. I missed a portion of it. I was in the kitchen and the TV was on in the living room." She paused and made a nervous sound. "But just to be sure, I called the Los Angeles Street Station where Joyce works, but they wouldn't answer any of my questions. They wouldn't tell me anything."

"What about Olivia? What about West? They work with the police, they—"

"My sister and West went out of town on some covert FBI case. I can't reach them, either."

"Hospitals," he said, starting to panic. "Did you try—"

"No, but I doubt they would give me any information. I'm not a relative."

He turned and nearly knocked over the lamp. He wasn't a relative, either. He was nothing to Joyce. Nothing but the man who'd made her cry.

"I'm trying not to overreact, not to think bad thoughts," Allie said. "But it's awful not to know what's going on."

"I'll find out." As soon as he could breathe, as soon as he quit envisioning Joyce with a bullet through her body. If something bad happened to her, he wouldn't survive. He wouldn't make it through another day. "I broke up with her. I walked away."

"Don't beat yourself up. You were just trying to cope with your feelings."

His forced the air from his lungs. "You and Olivia weren't pulling a matchmaking scam. Her prediction was real, wasn't it?"

"As real as a psychic reading can be."

But sometimes Olivia was wrong, he thought. Sometimes she made mistakes. There was no guarantee that what she said would come true.

Not if Joyce was dead, he told himself.

Not if he'd just lost the woman he loved.

Twelve

Kyle went crazy trying to find out if Joyce was safe. The first thing he did was call the network that had reported the shootings to get more information, but the lady who answered in the news department told him that she didn't have the capability of researching the story for him. He would have to call back in the morning when the network was fully staffed.

After that, he drove everywhere, all over the city, looking for answers. He entered the Los Angeles Street Station and inquired about Joyce in person, but the desk sergeant didn't appear to believe that he was Joyce's lover. The other man refused to share any information with him. Instead, the wary sergeant treated him as though he were a criminal stalking a cop.

Kyle tried to locate her partner, a detective he'd met eight months ago when he'd first met Joyce, but that was a dead end, too. There was no one at the station who could vouch for him, who knew he'd helped the police in the past.

From there, he drove to her parents' house, but they weren't home. To him, that was a major red flag. Where would her mom and dad be at this hour? Keeping vigil at their daughter's hospital bed? At the morgue, identifying her body?

There was nothing left to do but check hospitals and morgues himself. He spent hours going from place to place, battling the tightness in his stomach, looking for the lady he loved. But he didn't find her or her family.

He wasn't able to contact Joyce's sisters. He had no idea where they lived or what their phone numbers were. And since all of them were married, he didn't know their last names. Calling the local directory wouldn't help.

At daybreak, he sat in his car, wondering if he'd missed any hospitals. Los Angeles and the surrounding areas were filled with medical centers. He didn't know where the shooting had occurred and what facility the police officers had been taken to, but he'd gone to as many locations as he could.

The morgues he'd visited had left him cold, chilled straight to the bone. If Joyce was laid out on a slab somewhere, he hadn't been directed to her body.

At this point, he was lost, alone and confused. He called Allie to check in with her, then drove to Joyce's apartment.

What else could he do but go to her house and wait? Pray that she came home, that this nightmare was a mistake, that the report Allie had heard was flawed.

He used his key and went inside. The empty apartment gave him a ghostly feeling. He walked from room to room, then remained in her bedroom, where he lifted a perfume bottle from her vanity table.

The familiar fragrance made him ache.

He would do anything to hold her again, to take her in his arms and feel her heart beating next to his. He sat on the edge of her bed. It was neatly made, the pillows fluffed, the white quilt draped like a wedding dress.

Kyle knew he wanted to marry her. He knew, without a doubt, that he wanted her to be his wife.

For all the good it did. If she never came home, then his vow wouldn't matter. All that would be left was the night he'd left her standing alone in the dark.

The night he'd ended their relationship.

Too weary to think straight, he turned on the clock radio. The small black box came alive, sending music into the air. He found a station that was reporting the local news and listened intently, but they didn't mention the shootings.

Nothing. No update.

Exhausted, he turned it off, then flopped down and closed his eyes. If he fell asleep, would Joyce appear in his mind? Kyle wasn't a dream shaman. Even if he saw her in his subconscious, he wouldn't know what it meant.

Still, he wanted to see her. He wanted to be with her, as close as possible. Even if she wasn't real.

For him, it was better than not having her at all.

Butterflies lit upon Kyle's cheek. No, not butterflies. Fingertips. Someone was touching him, but only for a second.

He squinted in the misty morning light and saw the outline of a woman standing over him.

Was this the dream he'd been hoping for? "Joyce?" he said, wondering if she was an angel or a ghost.

"What are you doing here?" she responded.

"Waiting for you." Groggy, he struggled to clear the cobwebs from his mind. Her voice sounded distant, faraway.

His lover. The woman he feared was dead.

By now, his pulse was trembling. He clutched the quilt, afraid the room might spin, that she might disappear.

Confused, he sat up. "Is this actually happening? Are you real?"

"Of course, I am. You're in my apartment. What's going on?"

He took a deep breath, filling his lungs with oxygen. He wanted to grab her and never let go. But she seemed cautious, unsure of him.

"I thought something terrible happened to you." He explained everything, starting with Allie's phone call. "I've been so scared, Joyce. So worried."

She sat next to him. Her hair framed her face and her makeup was slightly mussed. He wanted to kiss her, but he knew it was too soon. She hadn't accepted him yet.

"I'm sorry," she said. "I saw that news report. But those officers weren't shot here. It happened in Northern California."

Which made sense, the reason he couldn't find any answers last night. "Do you know if they're okay?"

"The last I heard, they were both in stable condition." She brushed his knee, a barely there touch. "You look exhausted, Kyle."

"Can you blame me? How would you look if you thought I was dead?" He wished she trusted him enough to keep touching him, to make their connection more real. "Why couldn't I find you? Where were you?"

"I spent the night at Jessica's house. I've been

there for the past few days. My sister is helping me cope with…"

Her words faded into nothingness, but he knew what she meant. Joyce was hurting over their breakup, and he hated himself for what he'd done to her. "Your parents weren't home last night, either."

"They're on a holiday. Dad surprised Mom with an anniversary trip to Hawaii."

"Why didn't you answer your cell phone? Allie left messages and so did I." He paused, unable to clear the emotion from his voice. "I kept calling all night."

She made a troubled face. "I lost my phone. Or Owen lost it, I guess. He was playing 'police radio' with it and it disappeared. It's probably buried in Jessica's yard somewhere."

Suddenly Kyle couldn't help but smile, picturing her nephew leaving her phone in a pile of kid rubble.

A second later, his smile fell. "The cops at your station wouldn't tell me anything. They didn't believe that we dated. That I was your lover."

"I'm sorry. I never told my co-workers about you."

He understood. He hadn't told his Warrior Society about her, either.

In the next instant, they both fell silent. The moment turned awkward, and he didn't know what to say. Their affair seemed like a long, lost memory. Yet they'd made love less than a week ago.

Finally, she spoke. "Maybe you should call Allie. You should tell her I'm safe."

He agreed, using his cell phone, putting Allie's concerns to rest. Afterward, he gazed at Joyce. He was nervous about admitting that he loved her, nervous about saying the words out loud.

"Are you as mixed up as I am?" he asked.

She nodded, and he breathed a sigh of relief, grateful for her honesty. Relationships had never been easy for Kyle. He'd based his life on the mess his parents had made of theirs, on the hurt and pain his mother had endured. He never wanted to do that to a woman.

Never.

But he knew he wouldn't. Not if Joyce would give him a chance.

"I'm in love with you," he said, taking the fear-induced plunge.

She all but blinked at him. "Because you thought I died?"

"Yes. No. Sort of." His nerves kicked in again. He wasn't good at expressing himself, at exposing his heart. "I started figuring out how I felt before Allie called. Before I thought something happened to you."

"Are you sure?" Her voice vibrated. "Are you absolutely sure?"

"I've never been more for sure of anything in my life."

"I'm in love with you, too." Sunlight streamed into the room, making her hair seem more golden, her eyes more blue. "But how can we make it work? We're so different from each other."

"That shouldn't matter, Joyce."

"But it does. You know it does." She stalled for a moment. "Why do you carry a concealed weapon, Kyle?"

Her question caught him off guard. He wasn't armed. He'd left his SIG at home. "It's been my way of rebelling, I guess. Of being a modern-day warrior. But I won't carry a gun anymore." He smiled a little, making a silly joke, hoping to ease the tension. "Not unless you can help me get a permit."

She smiled too, but she didn't seem any calmer than he was. When she folded her hands on her lap, he noticed that some of her fingernails were chipped, splintered, as though she'd torn them purposely, as though it were an anxiety-ridden habit, something she struggled to control.

"I'm willing to make all sorts of changes," he said. "To compromise, to do whatever I have to do for us to be together."

"That's what I wanted you to say on the night you broke up with me. I wanted you to alter your lifestyle for me, but I don't know if that's fair, if it's right." Her eyes locked on his. "You are who you are."

He feared that he was losing her, that she would never marry him, never agree to be his wife. He frowned at her. "I just told you that I wasn't going to carry an illegal firearm anymore. That it isn't important."

"What about your missions? Stealing back stolen antiquities?" She held his gaze. "I could never condone that. Never accept it. But if you gave up your missions, you'd probably resent me for interfering."

"I don't have to give up my missions. I can pursue them legally. And you can help. You and the FBI. You already said you would."

She pushed the issue. "What about the other men in your Warrior Society? How are they going to feel about you being in love with a white cop?"

"They're going to think I'm nuts," he admitted. "But they already think I'm half-crazy anyway. And if they don't accept the woman I love, then they're not my friends. They're not the brotherhood I thought they were." He turned the conversation in her direction. "Maybe this is harder for you than it is for me. You've got your family and your job to consider. What would everyone think if you got engaged to a guy like me? If I became your husband?"

"My husband?" Her breath hitched. "Are you asking me to marry you?"

"Yes." His heart blasted his chest. He'd done it.

He'd just proposed to her. "I want us to have the baby Olivia predicted. I want a future with you."

"I want that, too." She gave into her emotions, letting her eyes water, letting him see what his words meant to her. "I've been fantasizing about you being my husband all along."

He reached for her. "Please tell me that's your way of saying yes."

She fell into his embrace, nearly crying in his arms. "Yes."

He nuzzled her hair. "Are we losing our minds, Detective Riggs?"

"Yes," she said again, making him laugh. "But I'm willing to compromise, too."

"To live with me and all of my junk? To tell your family and your co-workers that you're marrying a big, bad Apache?" He pulled her onto his lap, holding her gently, refusing to let go. "You've got your work cut out for you."

"My family likes you." She put her head on his shoulder. "And my co-workers will learn to accept you. If they don't, I'll kick their law enforcement butts."

"Listen to you. Tough girl."

"I've had a good trainer." She gave him a warm, willing kiss, showing him that she needed him as much as he needed her. "A big, bad Apache who changed my life."

* * *

On Halloween, Joyce and Kyle spent the evening at her apartment. She arranged a mixture of candy in a large glass bowl, and he carved a pumpkin, giving the jack-o-lantern a big, toothy smile.

She moved to stand beside him. There were squash innards all over the kitchen table. "He looks friendly."

"I don't want to scare the little kids who come to the door. And it's a she." He pointed to the marks above the rectangular eyes. "See? Long, pretty lashes."

She studied his handiwork. She couldn't have imagined a more perfect holiday, a more perfect man. He turned to kiss her, and she tugged on his shirt, keeping him close to her heart.

Suddenly Bonnie barked, nabbing their attention, dancing happily at their feet. Joyce picked up the little pooch and nuzzled her. She was dressed like an angel, with a doggie halo Kyle had found at a pet store.

She shifted her gaze to Clyde. The rottweiler wore a set of devil horns. But he didn't seem to mind. If anything, he took it in stride, accepting the silly costume as another aspect of his loyal duties.

She set Bonnie down and went over to Clyde, kneeling to scratch his chin. Now that he realized she was Kyle's lifelong mate, he'd warmed up to her.

Kyle illuminated the jack-o-lantern with a battery-operated device that looked like a candle. He placed the pumpkin outside, preparing for trick or treaters.

When he returned, he smiled at Joyce. "Have you thought of any names?"

She adjusted Clyde's horns. "Names?"

"For our daughter."

Her pulse fluttered. "It's too soon. I'm not anywhere near being pregnant."

"Yeah, but you will be. I threw away the condoms."

"*Kyle.*"

"Don't *Kyle* me. I'm pushing forty, too. If we're going to have kids, then we need to get started."

"Don't you think we should get married first?" she teased, even though they'd been planning their wedding. She wanted a formal ceremony, so he'd agreed to wear a tux, as long as the lapels were beaded with an Apache design. She thought it was a beautiful idea.

"Oh, that's right. I proposed, didn't I?" He walked over to her and removed a plastic container—the kind that held gumball prizes—from his pocket.

She stared at it. "What's that?"

"A ring."

Joyce didn't know what to expect, a real diamond or a fifty-cent treasure. With Kyle, a woman could never be sure.

She cracked open the case and found both: an engagement ring that nearly knocked her off her feet, and a toy ring that looked as hokey as hokey could get.

Dazzled, she leaped into his arms and kissed him breathless. He tasted like dreams and wishes and wild, crazy love.

After they separated, she put a ring on each hand. He checked out the bling-bling effect and grinned.

Heaven help her, but she adored this man and all of his romantic quirkiness. Their children were going to adore him, too.

The doorbell rang, and they answered it together, handing out candy to a group of dressed-up toddlers who'd arrived with their parents.

Bonnie peeked around the corner, making the little ones laugh. Clyde stayed out of sight, but he still wore his horns.

This was Joyce's family now—her future husband, his animated dogs and the babies they'd agreed to have.

Life with Kyle Prescott would never be boring.

She reached for his hand and linked her fingers through his, where they waited for another group of kids to climb the stairs. He leaned over to peck her cheek, and she realized how lucky they were.

Later that night, when the trick or treaters were gone and the pumpkin light was extinguished, they made love in her room, touching and kissing, whispering in the dark.

He roamed her body, and she reacted to his touch.

She arched to welcome him, to let him slide between her legs. He was hard and thick and desperately aroused.

But this was more than sex, more than an erotic joining. This was a man and a woman making a commitment, a vow that left her breathless.

Moonlight shimmered through the window, sending silvery streaks across the bed. This was the first time they'd made love without protection, without a veil of latex between them.

Flesh to flesh, she thought.

She ran her fingers up and down his spine. He moved inside her, a rhythm so deep, so real, she couldn't think beyond needing him, beyond accepting him as her mate.

She looked up at him, this man she was going to marry, this man who fought to change the world. She could feel the power of who he was, of what he believed in.

Together they would make a difference. Together, their limits were boundless.

Joyce didn't believe in fairy tales. She didn't believe in knights who swept ladies off their feet. But she believed in warriors who made compromises.

He lowered his head to kiss her, and their tongues tangled, the intensity of their lovemaking getting stronger.

Wilder.

They rolled over the bed, fever raging in their blood. Beautiful, sweet, reckless heat. It was part of them, part of what fueled their attraction.

But she couldn't imagine it any other way.

She craved the fire he ignited; she thrived on it, anxious for every sensation. He did exquisite things to her, making her heart pound gloriously in her breast, making her climax in his arms.

And when he spilled into her, she held him, knowing she would love him forever.

* * * * *

Watch for Allie's story,
NEVER LOOK BACK, available
February 2006 from Silhouette Bombshell.

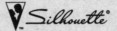

If you enjoyed what you just read,
then we've got an offer you can't resist!

Take 2 bestselling love stories FREE!

Plus get a FREE surprise gift!

Silhouette

Desire®

TEXAS
Cattleman's Club

THE SECRET DIARY

**A new drama unfolds for six
of the state's wealthiest bachelors.**

This newest installment continues with

ROUND-THE-CLOCK
TEMPTATION
by Michelle Celmer
(Silhouette Desire, #1683)

When Nita Windcroft is assigned a bodyguard,
she's determined to refuse. She needs an
investigator, not a protector. But one look
at Connor Thorne—a quiet challenge begging
to be solved—and she realizes that having him
around all the time is a sensual opportunity
she can't resist!

*Available October 2005
at your favorite retail outlet.*

COMING NEXT MONTH

#1681 THE HIGHEST BIDDER—Roxanne St. Claire
Dynasties: The Ashtons
A sexy millionaire bids on a most unlikely bachelorette and gets
the surprise of his life.

#1682 DANGER BECOMES YOU—Annette Broadrick
The Crenshaws of Texas
Two strangers find themselves snowbound and looking for ways
to stay warm, while staying out of danger.

#1683 ROUND-THE-CLOCK TEMPTATION—
Michele Celmer
Texas Cattleman's Club: The Secret Diary
This tough Texan bodyguard is offering his protection…day and
night!

#1684 A SCANDALOUS MELODY—Linda Conrad
The Gypsy Inheritance
She'll do anything to keep her family's business…even become
her enemy's mistress.

#1685 SECRET NIGHTS AT NINE OAKS—Amy J. Fetzer
When a wealthy recluse hides from the world, only one woman
can save him from his self-imposed exile.

#1686 WHEN THE LIGHTS GO DOWN—Heidi Betts
Plain Jane gets a makeover and a lover who wants to turn their
temporary tryst into a permanent arrangement.

SDCNM0905